THE PERFECT DISASTER

APPLEBOTTOM MATCHMAKER SOCIETY

ABBY TYLER

SUMMARY

When a newcomer to Applebottom with an untrained Great Dane wrecks several businesses in Town Square, the old-timers know exactly what to do. Match the young woman with their only hope for controlling the lovable 150-pound four-legged disaster -- the hunky football coach with a soft spot for dogs.

AbbyTyler
PO Box 160116
Austin, TX 78716
www.abbytyler.com

Paperback ISBN: 9781938150852

Edition 1.0

APPLEBOTTOM TOWN SQUARE PROPRIETORS
Gertrude Vogel, secretary
Because nobody else in town is literate.

Today we met at the Applebottom Pie Shoppe, owned by yours truly.

Maude Lewis, my nasty old co-owner, tried to cross out the *pe* at the end of *shoppe* in my notes and got purple ink on the sleeve of my brand-new Walmart blouse.

I told her to watch where she aimed that infernal pen, and she told me I shouldn't have gotten all fancy with the word *shoppe* and named our store a normal *shop* like a regular human.

I told *her* that our pie shop had been a *shoppe* since President Nixon and she just needed to get over it already.

She said she wished she'd made me change it when she bought half of it.

I told her I wished she'd just hush up about it.

We've been having this same argument since 1997.

Delilah Jones, owner of Nothing but a Pound Dog, butted in and reminded us to get back to the agenda. As if we had one.

Maude went to get a Tide stick for my blouse, and we poured another round of coffee while we waited for her to get back.

Our illustrious mayor T-Bone added a splash of whiskey to his coffee, but nobody said nothing about it, given that it's five o'clock somewhere.

I've been known to nip some of the bourbon we keep for the pecan pie any time that tall drink of water Alfred Felmont comes in to fetch a slice of lemon meringue, his favorite. Lord, that man makes me tongue-tied.

Maude came back and took another peek at my notes and told me I was too old to be sparking over Alfred Felmont. I nearly smacked her with my good leather notebook, except I have a high regard for our distinguished group and don't want to get blood on our minutes.

Delilah cleared her throat and plumped up her beehive, which is supposedly vintage retro style, but the only beehives around here are out on Grant Nelson's farm. With *bees* in them.

Delilah went on to tell us what transpired in her dog bakery.

A new girl named Ginny Page came trotting into town with a behemoth of a dog, a Great Dane she calls Roscoe. He outweighed the girl by a good bit, and she had zero control over him. Delilah had her door propped open to snatch some of the fall breeze (I told her she's going through *the change* but she doesn't believe me, they never do) and the dog dragged the girl right inside her store. He proceeded to ransack the place.

Topher and Danny Smith-Cole, who own Applebottom Blossoms, about jumped out of their chairs, hollering something about twisted gut syndrome and had anybody checked on the dog after he ate all that. But Delilah shushed them and said the dog was fine and just yesterday was seen dragging that poor girl down Main Street and almost causing three car accidents when he cut through traffic.

She insisted we had to do something, or she didn't dare open the doors to her own bakery lest the dog eat her out of house and home. Maude said she was out of order since it was her business and not her place of residence, and Delilah got huffy and her cheeks turned red, which is not a good look for a fifty-seven-year-old woman. Especially since she's obviously going through the change.

Danny said it was a shame we'd just lost Horace Shillings, the only dog trainer in Applebottom. He moved to Arkansas to a cabin in the Ozarks proper and was rumored to be a fan of the Razorbacks now.

Maude caught sight of my notes and *tut-tutted* in her ornery old way. But we were all in agreement that it's a sacred sin to switch teams like that. Danny and Topher got a good chuckle when I said it, and I don't know why, but I'm good for laughing when the laughing's good so I jumped right in.

Delilah insisted we do something, but nobody had any ideas. Maude asked who in town had any expertise in dogs, but most everybody we know has an animal they can control. Delilah suggested asking Savannah's help, but Maude said no, that poor girl has enough to manage out at the animal shelter with Boone so far out of health.

Danny said maybe we could just find someone strong enough to help her until she could teach it some commands. We all thought about it for a while, then Topher remembered that the football coach looked pretty strong and since he was single and all, he might have time to help her.

Betty Johnson, who runs Tea for Two, said he was a total hunk, and it was a shame no local girl had caught his eye in the two years he'd been coach.

And that settled it. Delilah said she'd send a book over to the girl on how to train your dog, and someone could call the high school and ask if the coach would help her out.

T-Bone pointed out it was football season and the

coach might be busy, but then everybody laughed because our team hasn't had a winning season since 1985 and they can't be practicing all that much.

We assigned the call to Topher, since his mother Sadie is the school secretary, and everybody got a slice of our newest creation, a cranberry-plum pie in honor of the coming season. Maude and I call it *Red Slice*.

Meeting adjourned.

CHAPTER 1

Ginny Page knew it would only be a matter of time before she got kicked out of town.

She gazed over at the source of all her problems.

He was handsome. Sweet. Adorable. And totally chill as he lay next to her on the grassy hillside of the public park. To make matters worse, every so often he would glance up, his gentle eyes meeting hers as if they were soulmates.

They sort of were.

He was so beautiful. Ginny's heart squeezed.

Except.

He wasn't always this great.

Looking at him, you would never know the incredible amount of destruction he brought upon Town Square just a few days ago. He'd become a crazed maniac. Tables overturned. Glass shattered.

His brazen dash through traffic almost caused three car accidents.

Ginny had moved to this tiny community of Applebottom, Missouri, only two weeks ago, yet she was already the talk of the town.

Maybe she'd make a mistake bringing him with her. She barely knew him.

Ginny stared too long at him, and he noticed. He lifted his snout and gave her a little *woof.*

"It's okay," she said. "There's nobody here to bother us."

She'd no more said it when a lanky teen boy approached their spot. Earbuds snaked from a hidden pocket in his jacket. He gave Ginny a nod. "Nice dog, lady."

Roscoe lifted his head as if considering whether or not he should pounce.

"Thank you," Ginny said carefully. She'd already learned not to sound too excited or that would set Roscoe off.

"What is he? A Great Dane?"

"Yes," she said. "About two years old."

"I think he's bigger than you."

"He outweighs me by a bit."

His gaze paused on the harness circling Ginny's waist and followed it up the line connecting it to the one around Roscoe's chest. "I sure wouldn't want to be strapped to him if he took off."

Ginny murmured noncommittally. She knew how it looked. She wouldn't have used the body harness if she could have safely taken Roscoe outside any other way.

The boy moved on, cresting the hill and disappearing over the other side.

Ginny let out a sigh. She never knew when she encountered a member of this small town if they'd already made a judgment about her and poor Roscoe. Ever since their disaster, she'd stayed away from Town Square and the shops.

But the job Ginny had moved for would start in two days, and the thought of meeting other people in town filled her with dread.

All because of her dog.

Roscoe was new to her. A month before she left Chicago, her best friend Celia found the emaciated Great Dane in a gutter behind her apartment complex. Celia had snuck the big dog inside. With the help of a vet, they got Roscoe cured of worms, free of parasites, and his back leg braced so it would heal properly.

Ginny had visited Roscoe several times while he steadily improved. He was such a sweet and gentle dog. Ginny would lie beside him in his big sheepskin bed, and he would sigh against her shoulder. Sometimes he whimpered a little if his pain medication had worn off.

Unfortunately, Celia's landlord discovered the

dog. She gave Celia ten days to find it a new home or she would be evicted.

Ginny felt a deep connection to him and panicked when Celia said she had to find him a home, or she would have no choice but to call a shelter. Ginny was moving within the week and paced her apartment, trying to decide if she could take him.

Her rented house in Missouri had a solid fence in the backyard, and it seemed like fate that Roscoe would come to her just as she made this big move.

So she'd brought him.

The wind kicked up another notch, lifting tendrils of hair from her forehead. It felt good in Applebottom. The weather was perfect, gentle and nourishing. The town was nestled at the foot of the Ozark mountains on the edge of Table Rock Lake, so the views were incredible.

It felt like home.

Or at least it had, until Roscoe trampled half of Town Square.

Ginny looked over at the dog. He slept again, an occasional snort breaking the quiet. He really was sweet. He just couldn't control himself. He hadn't been microchipped, so Ginny and Celia weren't sure how long he'd been on the streets or if he'd ever had a home.

Ginny's parents had never allowed her to have a dog growing up, so she had very little experience. Between packing, driving, then unpacking, she'd done the best she could to watch videos on training a dog to sit and heel and obey. The thing was, most of those dogs were normal size. Roscoe, to put it mildly, was *huge*.

Ginny hadn't known he was so excitable when she loaded him into her car for the three-day trek from Chicago to Missouri. In Celia's apartment, he'd been sleepy and cuddly, although his limp was quickly going away, and he was putting on weight in a hurry. Ginny had this false sense that he was calm and easygoing all the time.

A few hours into the drive, she'd stopped at a roadside rest spot so that Roscoe could do his business. She gave him a nice big meal and planned to walk him on the edge of the woods.

But being out of the city seemed to energize him. He took off running, trying to race the cars flying along the freeway. Ginny was caught surprised, and Roscoe managed to jerk the leash right out of her hands. She'd sprinted a good half-mile behind him before he finally paused for a breath, and Ginny was able to tackle him.

Just thinking about all the disasters she'd endured in their short time together made her cheeks burn, and Ginny was glad for the breeze to cool them down.

Roscoe let out another little *woof*, and her anxiety peaked. His head was up, his ears pricked.

"Steady, boy."

His nose sniffed the air. Ginny inhaled too, trying to figure out what might be interesting him. She kept her hand on the leash that connected them, her heart hammering painfully. This big lakeside park was the only place she would risk taking him after what had happened last week in town.

But maybe this had also been a mistake.

Finally, the smell hit her. Hot dogs. There was a vendor somewhere in the park. Roscoe lifted his boxy snout and sniffed again. Ginny got to her knees to brace herself in case he bolted.

"Let's go home, Roscoe," she crooned.

She slid her backpack over her shoulders. Roscoe stepped off the blanket, and Ginny slowly bent down to grab it. The trick was to talk calmly and make no sudden movements.

"Let's go home and get you a treat."

At the word *treat*, Roscoe leaped forward, tongue lolling out. He definitely understood that.

Ginny snatched up the blanket and turned toward home. Her rental house was only six blocks from the park. "This way, Roscoe. Come on. Let's go home."

Roscoe ignored her. His entire body vibrated. He was like a homing device, straining for the signal, locking in the coordinates of this luscious scent.

Ginny knew the moment he had it. He leapt like a racehorse coming out of the gate. For a split second, the leash remained slack between them. Then Ginny jerked forward.

"Roscoe!"

But there was no stopping him. He hurtled up the hill.

Ginny dropped the blanket, needing to be unencumbered as she tried to keep pace. Roscoe's run was slow and loping, so she managed to stay with him. When they reached the top, he slid to a halt. Thank goodness. Ginny bent over and sucked in a breath.

"Roscoe. Let's go home." She tugged on the leash to lead him away.

His nose remained lifted, four paws firmly planted. Ginny turned to survey the scene. A few parents sat on a bench, watching their children climb the monkey bars.

Then she spotted the problem. A man stood behind a folding table by one of the small grills that dotted this part of the park. A big white sign taped to it said, "Support the Eagle Band."

Roscoe and Ginny saw it at the exact same time. He strained forward. Ginny grasped the leash tethered between them and pulled him back.

The man forked a wiener and placed it inside a bun. He stuck it in a small white tray and passed it to a mom, who was managing twin toddler boys. For a moment, Ginny thought maybe it would be okay. Roscoe seemed content to observe the scene.

The mother squirted ketchup on the hot dog and passed it to one of the children. She accepted a second one, struggling with her bag and the boys as she got money to pay him.

Then the worst happened.

The boy dropped his hot dog on the ground.

Roscoe dipped low in front and let out an excited bark.

Oh no.

He took off down the hill, aiming straight for the hot dog at the foot of the upset boy. Ginny reached for the leash to brace herself against his weight, but the dog had too much momentum. She flew forward, arcing through the air as if she had just taken a dive into a pool.

Right as she was about to face plant into the grass to be dragged across the park, strong arms encircled her body. While one held on to her, the other deftly wrapped itself around Roscoe's leash and pulled.

The two of them clasped together outweighed her dog. The harness held, and Roscoe jerked to a stop partway down the hill. He planted his back paws and tried to leap forward again, but they had him.

Roscoe turned to look at Ginny as if to say *what gives?*

The man holding Ginny said, "He's a wild one. I see why Delilah sent me."

"Someone sent you?"

The stranger released her and used the leash to slowly reel in the dog. Roscoe seemed to recognize that he was outmatched at the moment. He gazed longingly back at the table. The seller, blissfully unaware of the near disaster, had given the young boy a new hot dog. As the mother walked away, he circled the table and picked up the one that had dropped.

"Let's get away from that tantalizing smell," said the mystery man. He kept his arm wrapped around the leash between her waist harness and Roscoe's. Together they wrestled Roscoe over the hill to the safer side.

"That yours?" he asked as they passed the blanket.

"Yes." Ginny still felt a little dazed by the events of the last ninety seconds. Her head wasn't screwed back on yet.

The man leaned down and scooped up the blanket. Who was this guy?

Now that they were more or less settled, Ginny really took him in. He was a whole head taller than her. Light brown hair. A ridiculously muscular build. He must spend a lot of time at the gym.

He wore an Eagles High School T-shirt and gray workout shorts, but he was definitely too old to be a student. He led them toward the walking path along the lake. Ginny generally avoided this area because Roscoe lunged forward at the sight of every human. If he saw another dog, the peril of being dragged loomed very real.

But this man seemed to have the situation well in

hand. Roscoe trotted along beside them as if he'd just finished obedience school.

"You're Ginny, right? I didn't think there would be any other beautiful girls with an oversized dog in Applebottom Park."

Her face flushed at the word *beautiful*. Was that his word or someone else's?

"Yes, I'm Ginny. Who did you say sent you?"

"Delilah. The beehive lady who owns the dog bakery."

Great. So this guy knew all about what happened. Probably everybody did. "Roscoe went a little crazy in her store a few days ago."

"I don't have any details," he said. "I was just told to find you, that you were down here, and this was a good time."

Did everybody watch everyone else around here? Not surprising. A newcomer was probably already fascinating, and Roscoe made them qualify as a circus freak show.

He switched hands that held onto the leash and extended his right one. "I'm Carter. I coach football at the high school. I hear you're starting at the elementary school on Monday."

Ginny shook his hand, warm and strong. A little zip went through her.

"Yes. Seems they finally got a budget for an occupational therapist."

"It was quite the effort of the town to figure out a

way to pay for that," he said. "Everyone is dying to meet you."

Except the ones who already had.

Ginny brushed loose bits of hair out of her face. Her ponytail was definitely the worse for wear after the mad dash. "I've been up to the school a couple times to set up the room."

"I've seen it," he said. "It's amazing."

She cocked her head at him. "Will some of the football players be coming to me at the elementary?"

"I don't think so, but I hear you'll be at the high school on Fridays."

"They're still looking for a space for me to set up. The school is full?"

He nodded. "We have a bigger senior class than usual. Thirty-seven." He laughed. "I guess that seems small to someone from Chicago."

"My graduating class was six hundred."

He whistled. "I bet you didn't know them all."

"Not even close."

The wind rustled the trees, catching their attention.

"Hello, autumn," he said. "Can't wait for the leaves to turn. They'll start falling in a few weeks."

"It's already chilly in Chicago," Ginny said. "I'm not going to miss that extended winter."

"This weather is going to be a dream compared to that."

"I guess I'm going to find out." They grinned at

each other, and despite everything that had happened in Applebottom since Ginny had arrived, she felt this incredible surge of hope. This had been the right move. Uproot herself. Escape the city and get out of the rat race. She'd spent the last two years dashing from one part of town to the other, seeing kids in their homes.

Now she had a room of her own. The students wouldn't change every few months, but be the same all year long. She could really track their progress. Her life felt full of purpose.

And of course, now there was Carter.

CHAPTER 2

Carter McBride walked alongside this newcomer and tried to manage the unexpected optimism that had overcome him since he'd spotted Ginny and her dog.

The dirt crunched beneath their feet, and the trees arched overhead. They had talked about nothing more important than the weather, but Carter felt oddly at home.

He hadn't felt this comfortable around a woman in a long time. He hadn't let himself, not after his last humiliation.

The Great Dane ambled contentedly alongside them. Carter kept a strong grip on the harness, still not sure what to think of the big beast. He'd nearly dragged this girl across the park on her belly.

Delilah had been right. Ginny needed help with her dog.

"So how's the team looking this year, Coach?" Ginny asked.

Carter wanted to laugh. This was way more of a contentious subject than she knew. "We have a freshman quarterback with some promise," he said. "My hope is to score more than fourteen points."

"That's a good goal for a game," Ginny said.

He had to smile at that. She had no idea about Applebottom's losing tradition, one that began long before he arrived.

"I mean fourteen points in the *season*."

"Oh."

Now she got it.

"It's not a complaint," he said. "I love it here. I'm from Branson. The pace in Applebottom is much slower, and I can head over the lake anytime I want to return to a bigger city."

"I heard they have an amazing Titanic Museum," Ginny said. "I loved the movie, but I don't want to see a bunch of gimmicks."

"It's the real deal. You should go."

Because he had such a tight grip on the dog, he immediately noticed when Roscoe's pace faltered. He'd seen something. Carter braced his arm against his side to make sure he could hold the Great Dane if he bolted.

"Oh!" Ginny said.

Carter looked up. Betty Johnson, the seventy-year-old owner of the Town Square tea shop, approached with her little white poodle, Clementine.

"Watch out," Ginny said. "Roscoe gets a little excited around other dogs. He might take off."

Carter was already aware of Roscoe's intention. He'd stopped dead, straining forward to look at the little dog.

"I've got him," Carter said. Betty and Clementine were still well up the path. "So what's the deal with this dog? You never trained him?"

"I only got him a few weeks ago," Ginny said. Her face registered concern as Roscoe strained harder against the leash. "My friend found him starving and scrawny behind her apartment complex, but her landlord threatened to evict her. So I took him."

Carter coaxed Roscoe into a slow walk. The three of them had to stick pretty close together for Carter to remain an intermediary between the dog and Ginny with the harness connecting them. It took all of his focus not to bump into Ginny as he tried to keep the dog at bay.

"Let me guess," he said. "He got hale and hearty and was no longer the sweet rug dog you'd gotten to know."

Ginny had her eye on the approaching poodle. "Exactly. By then I was on my way here, away from any trainers or obedience schools. I've searched, but there's nothing here."

"There's bound to be some in Branson."

"There are. But after that epic drive down, Roscoe won't get in the car again. He's too big for me to force him."

"That's a problem for sure."

When Betty got close, little Clementine put on her doggy brakes. Carter could see her tiny legs shaking. Betty tugged gently on the leash. "Come along, Clementine," she cajoled.

Carter and Ginny halted with Roscoe as well.

"We can step off the trail," Carter said.

"Don't worry yourself," Betty said. She bent down and scooped up the tiny white poodle. The dog's pink bows exactly matched Betty's jogging suit. "She's just fine. She thinks this enormous guy could eat her in a single bite."

"He's a big one, for sure," Carter said.

Betty's clear blue eyes rested on Ginny. "I see you found her."

So the whole town *did* know about this meeting. Carter had figured that would be the case. Delilah had contacted Sadie Cole, the high school secretary, who tracked Carter down. If Delilah was involved, probably the whole Town Square society had talked about it. Betty was part of that. Not much happened in Applebottom that those ladies missed.

"Just in the nick of time," Carter said. "Joe was down there selling hot dogs for the band fundraiser, and Roscoe was ready to clean him out."

"Oh, I bet that was tempting." Betty turned to

Ginny. "I'm Betty. I own Tea for Two, the little sand-wich shop on the square. Near the doggy bakery that your pup visited recently."

Ginny's cheeks brightened to pink. "I'm so sorry," she said.

Betty waved her hand to dismiss the apology. "We all talked about it, and we decided Carter was the best solution. I'm glad he found you. Have a good one."

Carter kept Roscoe close, his fingers gripping his harness as Betty and Clementine passed. When she was out of earshot, Ginny said, "This is humiliating. Everybody knows."

He couldn't blame her for feeling that way. The Applebottom society women were a lot to manage. But he didn't want to discourage her. "Just know that the whole town is ready to welcome you and solve your problem."

"So they sent me you."

Carter crossed his free hand over his heart. "And I most solemnly swear to help out wherever I can."

And he meant it. Seeking out a young single woman wasn't something he would've done on his own. But if he had to help her with the dog, well, that was just neighborly.

"You have any experience with giant dogs?" Ginny asked.

"Not a bit. My mom strictly got us Pomeranians. They fit in my her purse."

"So it sounds like you and I will be figuring this out together."

"We will indeed." Carter couldn't help but grin at her as they moved forward to finish out the walking path. Roscoe had probably seen enough action for today. Carter steered them toward Ginny's street.

"You know where I live?" she asked, then quickly added, "Of course you do. I'm sure everyone here knows everything."

"I'd say that's pretty much the way of it." They turned down her road. His beat-up red pickup was parked in front of her house.

"That yours?" Ginny asked.

"Every rusting bit."

"Thanks for helping me out back there," Ginny said. "I never know what's going to trigger Roscoe." When they reached her porch, Roscoe sat on his haunches like a perfectly behaved dog.

"He knows a few things," Carter said. "We just have to get you some commands, so he'll obey you. The team doesn't practice after school on Tuesdays. You want to meet then?"

It was his only weeknight off, but he didn't mind spending it this way. The dog presented a fun challenge. And then there was the girl.

Ginny tucked a piece of stray hair behind her ear. She was definitely pretty, and he liked how straightforward she was. She didn't put on an act or try to snag him.

He'd had a heckuva time his first year in Apple-bottom, trying to manage the expectations of all the single women in town. He gone out with a few of them. But nothing seemed quite right. And in a town this small, he couldn't let things get too far without having a trove of local citizens advising him about the appropriateness of his behavior.

Ginny was different. She seemed mainly concerned about getting control of her dog. He could help her with that.

Carter scooped up the package he'd left on her door before he set out to find her. "Delilah sent me with a gift. I left it here in case I couldn't find you."

Ginny took the little bag, peering inside. "It's a dog training book and a bag of treats!"

"Subtle, that Delilah."

"We did sort of destroy her store."

"Back at the park on Tuesday? Five o'clock?" Carter asked.

"I'll be there."

Roscoe let out a little *woof*.

"We'll *both* be there," she added.

They laughed, and Carter found that he actually looked forward to Tuesday and the challenge of the dog.

And of course, Ginny too.

CHAPTER 3

Ginny arrived in her classroom on the first day of school ridiculously early. She'd been there all week setting up.

Today, though, everything felt different. The halls buzzed with teachers doing their last-minute prep. She'd passed the principal organizing the crossing guards, who were already ushering the earliest drop-offs into the cafeteria.

Ginny would no longer be alone in the room opening boxes of equipment and arranging the space. Actual students would arrive. She would begin her real work.

She took a moment to walk around and touch everything, pleased with how it had turned out. The floor was carpeted to absorb sound. In one corner, she'd arranged mats and cushions of different heights and shapes to be a sensory walk. In the opposite corner, a clear space left room for a large body-sized swing. Students who needed extra vestibular stimulation would use it to get calm and hopefully return to class ready to learn.

A circle of inflated ball chairs filled the center of the room, each on a nubby mat that kept them in place. The kids could bounce and shift and move their bodies on them while they listened to instructions.

Along the back wall were bright green cabinets filled with all the smaller tools she would use in specific cases. One was filled with sand-filled balls made expressly for children who tended to get their aggression out by throwing things. Three targets were painted on one wall for them to aim at. It was definitely better than flinging chairs or scissors, incidents that had been reported more than once last year.

Ginny's heart filled with hope that she could help all these kids, who apparently needed her desperately enough that the town had funded an endowment for an occupational therapy position. She was lucky, and she knew it.

A voice at the door got her attention. "Hello?"

She turned. It was Carly, one of the special education teachers Ginny had met when the school interviewed her. Carly had only recently returned from a vacation in Italy, so Ginny hadn't seen her while she was setting up.

"Hey!" Ginny said.

Carly wore the professional dress of a teacher who wanted to look nice even though she did plenty of manual labor with her students. Stretchy pants with a fitted top, tennis shoes, and a ponytail. She wasn't much older than Ginny—maybe thirty—with a bright, happy expression.

"This looks amazing," she said. "I can't wait to bring my kids in here."

"I can't wait to meet them."

Carly held out her hand. "I don't know if you remember me. I was there at your interview."

"I remember. Thank you for hiring me. I'm extremely excited to start."

"So are we. You're literally the answer to a lot of parents' and teachers' prayers."

Ginny hoped she could live up to that. "How was Italy?"

Carly let out a long sigh. "Perfect. Even more perfect because my parents paid for it. I think they just wanted an excuse to have the baby to themselves."

"How old is your little one?"

"Sixteen months. And a pistol. Running all over the place and causing trouble." She sat on one of the balance balls and bounced a few times, her ponytail swinging. "I might have to come in here to calm myself down."

Ginny laughed. "Feel free."

Carly stood up from the ball. "You know where I am if you need me, right? Two doors down, opposite side of the hall."

"I do."

"You may not have a whole lot of students the first couple of days," she said. "We have to get the schedule established first. You know, the routines."

"That makes sense," Ginny said, although this meant it might be a long, slow day.

"Just be available. There will be a few meltdowns, and we might bring them here. Some kids won't be emotionally ready to handle the rigors of a full day away from home. You'll get to know them pretty fast."

Ginny nodded. "Thanks. I've got everyone's files. And I have most of them memorized anyway."

"Good. I think you'll really like it here. Apple-bottom is a tight community. Everyone knows every-one, and most of the time they're here to help."

Most of the time.

Carly paused by the door and looked back. "I heard you met our football coach. Isn't he something?"

Ginny stared at her shoes. "He was nice."

"Nice!" She laughed. "He's been on every single woman's list since he showed up. But no takers."

"Really?"

"I don't know what he's looking for, but they're not it."

"He's just helping me with my dog."

"Sure he is." Carly winked.

The noise level suddenly rose in the hall. "Uh oh, they've released the assembly," Carly said. "To the trenches. Have a great first day!"

Carly hurried out. Voices and footsteps echoed down the hall. Soon it became a cacophony. Ginny moved out to the hallway, directing parents and lost kids in the right direction, glad she had walked the halls enough to know where things were. A couple mothers came up to introduce themselves, and Ginny recognized their children's names, thrilled to finally be able to connect their actual presence with their documentation.

An energetic woman in yoga pants and a fleece vest embraced Ginny in a tight hug. "I can't believe we actually got you," she said. "I think you're going to make all the difference in my son."

Ginny glanced down at her boy, about nine, wearing oversized headphones to muffle sound. He bounced on his toes, his eyes darting left and right.

"Is this Mason?"

"It is!" Her eyes sparkled that Ginny knew his name.

Ginny kneeled to his eye level. "I'm Miss Page. I'll be seeing you soon."

Mason's eyes swept her for only a moment, but Ginny knew he'd taken in everything he needed to know. She was already formulating activities in her head to help him with his visual scanning, stims that could feed his need for sensory input so that he could pay attention but not disrupt others. He was close to being mainstreamed. Maybe she could be the one to push him over the threshold.

As the halls quieted, and the children settled in their rooms, Ginny retreated to her own space and thought about what the mom said.

Make a difference. Was that true? In the six years that she had worked as an occupational therapist, she never felt like she had done much to help any of the children in her care.

The caseloads came and went, and authorizations were lost and revoked and reassigned to new people in an ever-spinning whirl of paperwork and faces. Ginny had seen only a few of the children make any progress at all.

Much of the time she'd felt her job revolved around keeping the child on her client list, as much as actually creating a lasting change in their bodies or skills. With any luck, this would be a new start for her as well as kids like Mason.

CHAPTER 4

On Tuesday, Ginny had no idea what to wear to a meeting where a handsome football coach would help her tame a dog. She'd chosen her favorite tracksuit that morning, thinking she would wear it throughout the rest of the day and to the dog lesson.

She didn't want to change, since no doubt the whole town was watching and would think she had dressed up after school in order to impress him. But Ginny also didn't want to read too much into this whole event. He really was just trying to help.

But by the time Ginny got home to happy barks and licks from Roscoe, her outfit had to go. That morning, a preschooler learning to use a spoon had gotten applesauce all down one sleeve. Then she'd spent more time than expected on her knees trying to coax seven-year-old Anna to come out of a play tunnel, leaving dark splotches on the front of the pants.

Since the training session with Roscoe would theoretically take less effort than an average day at work, Ginny slid into her favorite pair of jeans and a soft blue sweater. She rolled a light windbreaker into a tight bundle and stuffed it in the outside pocket of her backpack in case the weather cooled off while they were out.

Ginny carefully stowed Delilah's book, the treats, a water bowl, and all of the harnesses and leases she had acquired in the last few weeks. She still wasn't brave enough to simply hold the leash as she walked Roscoe, so she strapped on the body harness and tethered the line between her waist and her dog.

Roscoe was anxious to stretch his legs after being cooped up in the house. With Ginny's wonky schedule, she only got a few minutes for lunch, but she was able to come home during the longer break each day to let him race around the backyard. Thankfully the school was close.

But clearly Roscoe wanted more than the yard, even as large as it was. He tried to break into a trot, and Ginny gave him the command to walk. He didn't know it yet, but they had to start somewhere.

The tone of her voice seemed to register, though, and he slowed his pace. Ginny should have had a treat prepared for him to reward him for his obedience, but she didn't want to risk trying to get one now. If he got too excited about the bag, he might jump her, or grab it and take off. Rewards would have to wait for a more controlled situation at the park.

With a strong coach to help.

Ginny's inner tween giggled at the thought of meeting a *boy*. It wasn't that she hadn't dated before. She was twenty-eight years old, and there had been plenty of contenders. Just none of them had worked out.

First had been Jake, a two-year steady boyfriend in high school. They separated when he left for the University of Southern California. A string of short-lived romances in college filled out a couple more years, and then she met the guy everyone thought for sure was the *one*. Matthew.

They had dated exclusively. He would finish a year after her, so Ginny stuck to Chicago so they could remain together. She thought they had an understanding that he would also stay in Chicago for their future together.

But when his graduation day arrived, he accepted a position in New York. He never proposed or even asked if Ginny wanted to move with him. And in the end, she didn't care enough to pursue it. Her heart wasn't broken, and that told her all she needed to know.

Besides, Ginny had a job in her field, which was something many of her college friends struggled with. As they languished in retail or temporary positions, Ginny was hired by a therapy company that provided services inside homes, mostly to patients who were on federal assistance.

By the time Matthew left town, Ginny had been with the company long enough to realize how much she loved working with these kids to help them make the most of their skills. But not long enough to realize that her caseload would never settle, and she would only be a transient influence on their achievements.

Since then, she'd tried to fit in some dating with her exhausting workload and regular trips to Seattle to visit her parents. Mostly, though, she hadn't found anyone worth breaking her routine for.

Sometimes Ginny wondered if she'd made a mistake in not forcing a conversation after Matthew announced his new job. But that was long ago now.

She was here in Applebottom.

About to meet the football coach.

Ginny turned onto the street that led to the park. She didn't shift over to the walking trail, as she had done with Carter. Roscoe was too unpredictable. She'd rather not have their second meeting start off with another situation where she had to be saved.

In his usual fashion, Roscoe half-pulled, half-dragged her from one interesting-smelling spot to the next. At least traffic in Applebottom was minimal, so their zigzagging across the street so that he could sniff or pee on every tree and mailbox post wasn't something that would place her in mortal danger.

As they approached the base of the hill that had caused her so much trouble three days ago, Ginny spotted a figure sitting at the peak. She was pretty sure it was Carter, his knees up, his elbows resting on them. He looked the other way, across the children's park and to the lake's edge.

He was beautiful and strong and contemplative. Her heart sped up. Carly had said he hadn't really dated anyone in the two years he had been here. Ginny wondered why. Maybe there weren't so many prospects.

Or maybe he had been waiting for her.

Carter turned when a bark echoed across the park.

Roscoe and Ginny climbed up the rise.

The pair were almost comical. Roscoe's head reached chest level on her. She was so petite, and her dog was monstrous.

Carter stood up and dusted grass and leaves off his workout shorts. He hadn't put much thought into his outfit, an Eagles high school sweatshirt and tennis shoes. Seeing Ginny's pretty sweater and happy expression as she caught sight of him, he realized he should have at least put on some jeans.

Too late now.

"Carter!" she called.

"Hey."

Roscoe bounded up to him, placing his paws on Carter's shoulders. How did Ginny ever think she could control him?

"Hey, Roscoe," Carter said. "You look happy to see me." He accepted several long licks, then grasped Roscoe's paws and carefully set him down.

"Down, boy," he said. When Roscoe stayed down, he patted his head. "Good boy."

"I swear this dog behaves better for you than for me," Ginny said.

"What have you been working on with him?" Carter asked.

"Just the basics. We started with *sit* and *stay*, because according to the book Delilah sent, those are the foundation of everything else." Ginny grasped the tether between her waist and Roscoe's harness. Carter remembered how she'd sailed through the air the first time they met and hoped they could get the dog on a normal leash soon.

"Makes sense," he said. "What should we do first?"

Roscoe's nose lifted, and he made a sudden lunge. Carter grabbed the tether and held it taut before Roscoe could pull Ginny down.

"I say we work on *sit* for a while," she said, pressing her hand to her heart after the close call. "He does it sporadically, as if maybe he understands what I'm saying but he just doesn't want to do it."

"Sounds good." Carter looked around. "Are we sure this is the best spot?"

The broad view of the park, the water, and the trail probably wasn't the best choice. Roscoe could get distracted by anything that approached from any direction.

"I know a place." He gestured toward the trees.

"In the forest?"

"Something like that."

They descended the hill and moved into the tree line. The cedars stood tight and close until they reached a clearing with a cut path leading out the other side.

"What used to be here?" Ginny asked.

"A house," Carter said. "One of the early cabins of Applebottom. It collapsed decades ago and they hauled it all out."

"Too bad it wasn't preserved."

"The true originals have been. This was just one of the latecomers." Carter laughed. "If you're not born of one of the original settlers, you don't count as a native."

"Harsh."

"It's a fun bunch that runs the town. Delilah's family has been here for three generations, and she's still considered an interloper."

"Good thing I didn't upset a true pioneer. Did they come on the Mayflower and hike over?"

Carter laughed. "Everybody's going to love you."

"Not if I don't get a good handle on Roscoe."

"That's what I'm here for."

They stopped in the center of the clearing. Carter stepped close and reached for Ginny's waist to unhook the tether. He caught a whiff of something light and floral, not perfume, but lotion maybe. He liked it.

He wrapped the tether around his wrist. Ginny let out a sigh as if a great weight had been lifted now that he had control of the dog.

Roscoe stood tall and alert, his nose lifted. The evening sun slanted through the trees, casting long shadows. In the circle clearing, the rest of the town completely out of sight, they could be the only three creatures left in the world.

Carter might be okay with that.

"You want to tell him to sit?" he asked. "See if it works?"

"Sure." Ginny turned to Roscoe. "The book said to always say the dog's name first to make sure you had his attention."

"Give it a go."

Ginny looked down at her dog. "Roscoe, sit."

He didn't even turn his head.

"Try again."

"Roscoe, *sit.*"

Still nothing. Roscoe took a step toward the trees on the far side, his attention focused on a bird flitting from branch to branch.

"How well does he know his name?" Carter asked.

"I thought he did. But my friend gave it to him. He didn't have a collar or anything, so if he had some other name, we wouldn't know."

"How old is he?"

"The vet estimated that he was two."

Carter nodded. "Hey, Roscoe."

In true annoying-dog fashion, Roscoe turned to look.

"Why does he behave better for you?" she asked.

"I'm bigger than he is. It's the way of the pack."

"So you're the alpha."

He grinned at her and noted that she was staring at his lips. He itched with the temptation to kiss her.

But no, they had to focus.

Ginny broke her gaze and walked in front of Roscoe. "Hey!" she said, getting him to look at her. "Roscoe!"

The dog tilted his head.

"Roscoe," she repeated.

He sat down.

Carter fought to control his smile. "He seems a little mixed up."

"So I guess I have to make sure he knows his name first?"

"What does the book say about that?"

"I don't know. I just know that I'm not supposed to push on his butt to make him sit, or he won't get it."

Carter frowned. "I guess we can just walk in circles. I seem to recall when we would walk PomPom, if he'd try to get ahead of us, Mom would stop and make him come back to us before we would move forward."

"PomPom?"

"I didn't name that one," Carter said. "My baby sister did."

"Say it again." Ginny tried to hide her open-mouth laugh behind her hand.

"Say what?'

"Your dog's name."

He gave her a squinty-eyed glare. "PomPom."

She couldn't handle it. Apparently the name hit her funny bone so hard that her whole body started shaking.

"PomPom," he said again, just to keep her going. "PomPom. PomPom."

Ginny bent over, clutching her middle. "Okay, stop! Stop!"

"PomPom!"

She couldn't catch her breath. Roscoe realized something was up and began barking and leaping in the air.

"You're making him crazy," Carter said.

"Then...don't...say..."

"Say what? PomPom?"

Ginny waved her hand at him. "No…no more."

Roscoe strode up and stuck his nose into her chest. He whined, low and concerned.

"Okay, okay. I'm okay, Roscoe," she said. "It's all right."

She looked up at Carter, and he mouthed *PomPom*.

"Mercy. I give. No more."

Carter couldn't stop grinning. But he gave her a rest. "Roscoe," he said, hoping to solidify the dog's awareness of his name. "Roscoe." He petted his head.

Ginny followed suit, slowly regaining control over her laughter. "Roscoe. Roscoe." She petted him, too.

For the next several minutes, they only said the dog's name, combined with lavish attention.

"Maybe we should keep our talking to a minimum," Ginny said. "Only say the things that Roscoe needs to hear."

"I think it's more about tone," Carter said. "Like we have this one sort of quiet way of talking to each other, and then we have the different tone of voice to tell Roscoe that we need his attention."

"That makes sense," she said. "Because he's definitely not paying attention to us now." Roscoe's nose moved from side to side, sniffing the air. His every movement caused a flurry in the trees.

Carter couldn't blame the other critters. He

would be wary of a creature this size. "Roscoe," he said firmly. "Sit."

Roscoe's big brown eyes held Carter's for a moment, then he turned away.

"I still feel like that was progress," Carter said. "He looked at me when I called his name in that tone."

"Roscoe," Ginny said softly. He didn't turn his head. "Roscoe!" she said in a deeper, more firm voice.

Roscoe's head whipped around.

"He's getting it," Carter said. "Look at that."

The three of them walked the perimeter of the clearing, talking in a normal voice, then calling to Roscoe in the deeper tone. Each time Roscoe looked up when they said his name, Ginny fed him a treat.

"That went pretty well, don't you think?" Carter asked.

"It was eye-opening," Ginny said. "I won't be taking him to Town Square anytime soon, but at least we can be sure he'll understand when we're speaking to him."

Roscoe collapsed in the grass. He seemed weary of his lesson.

"We should get this big lug to your house," Carter said. "How do you make him move when he doesn't want to go somewhere?"

"It hasn't come up. He's always eager to go outside and walk with me. Otherwise, we are very much homebodies until he is trained."

"Well, I hope we can get you out of the house," he said. "The first home game is Friday."

"I'm sure I'll be there."

"Then I'll look for you." The words were out before he could stop them. Were they too much?

But Ginny simply said, "Okay." She pulled a treat out of a bag and waved it at Roscoe.

"Roscoe," she said. "Come."

Roscoe took several steps forward so Ginny was able to lure him back through the trees to the street.

"Look at that," Carter said. "He can be bribed."

"Thank goodness."

They headed to Ginny's house, side by side, the dog between them, and Carter marveled at how easy the walk was. How simple.

It felt right.

CHAPTER 5

Friday was more exciting than Ginny anticipated. The first football game meant a pep rally, so the elementary school sent all of their students to the high school to cheer the team.

Ginny had dropped into the high school only once before school started, to meet the principal and the special education coordinator. The campus was short on space, and they hadn't decided where to put her to meet with the teens who needed her on Friday afternoons.

Just yesterday, she'd gotten word that she would be temporarily placed inside the boys' locker room, which was unoccupied during the last three hours of the day when the girls took over the gym.

Ginny checked in with the front office, and a friendly older woman brightened when Ginny told her she was headed to the locker rooms. She intro-duced herself as the school secretary, Sadie Cole.

Sadie wore tons of bright jewelry that set off her pale red hair, accented with a bright red flower. She winked as she asked, "Hoping to catch a peek at Carter? How are the dog lessons going?"

Everybody *did* know everything. "We've just had one so far. It went well, though."

"Delilah sure is hoping it will work. I think she lives in fear of you guys trotting down Main Street again."

Ginny's cheeks burned. "I've been keeping Roscoe at home until I can manage him better. When we do go out, we stick to the park."

"I'm sure the two of you will get him in tip-top shape in no time. Do you know where you're going?"

"Not completely. I know where the gym is. I assume the dressing rooms are near there?"

"When you walk in, the girls' is the far left corner, and the boys are in the far right corner."

"Thank you."

"Anytime!" She looked Ginny up and down, as if assessing Ginny's ability to interest Carter when no one else had.

Ginny did hope she bumped into Carter. They hadn't set up a time to meet for another dog lesson, but they hadn't exchanged numbers or anything either. Ginny had no way to reach him unless she went through the school. Which meant Sadie would know.

She entered the gym to the clipped synchronized cheers of a group of girls rehearsing for the pep rally. The smell of leather and sports equipment, and the echoes of the girls' voices, made Ginny nostalgic for her own high school days. Fridays would a fun break from her elementary school routine.

She headed toward the boys' locker room. Ginny assumed that since the gym was devoid of boys, the dressing room would be as well. But she didn't take any chances and rapped carefully on the door. There was no answer. She opened it a crack and called inside. "Everyone decent?"

Still nothing. She risked a peek. The first section of the room held mats, balls, and other equipment. But no people.

As Ginny stepped inside, she wondered if this was the room that they were thinking of. With its open floor, she could make it work. She just needed to make sure her kids stayed out of the equipment. Some of it didn't look very secure, including an entire barrel full of wooden baseball bats. Hmm. Given the explosive behavior of some of the cases on her roster, maybe not.

The thought of trying to lug a bunch of equipment all the way through the school every Friday sounded problematic. Maybe if she could spare any extras from her room, she could find a place here to stash them. The inflatable balls alone were too much to shove in her car and bounce down the halls.

She spotted a door at the back of the room. A slice of light came through the crack, so she approached it cautiously. She didn't want to unexpectedly encounter the showers with anyone in them.

"Hello?" She took a few timid steps, relieved to see offices lining a narrow hall. These must be for the coaches. She moved closer, realizing it was too quiet for there to be any kids.

One of the doors had a metal plaque that read *Carter McBride*. Ginny touched it for a moment, conjuring his image, the sandy brown hair, the kind expression. He was something. Probably every teen girl had a crush on him. Was that hard for him to manage?

"Did you need me for something?"

Ginny jumped at the voice and whirled around. Of course it was Carter. Right as she was caressing his nameplate.

"Oh! No! Actually, I was just trying to figure out the spot where they thought I might be setting up on Fridays."

"They want to put you in the boys' locker room?"

"That's what I heard. It seems a little crazy. But maybe the open area with the equipment would work?"

"I'll have to check on that," he said. "You know there are guys who get dressed back here, right?"

"They said that the end of the day on Fridays were generally empty."

Carter rubbed his chin. "Yes, I suppose that's when the girls take over."

He was more dressed up than the other two times Ginny had seen him, in khaki pants and a red polo shirt with the Eagles logo embroidered on the pocket.

"Do you think they meant the front room? I'm concerned about the equipment."

"No telling," he said as he checked his watch. "I only have a second, but we could certainly take a quick walk around. You might see something the others don't."

They passed through another set of doors. "Back here is the main dressing area."

Half-size lockers lined the walls, and a pair of benches stood a few feet from each side. The main part of the floor was open.

"Do you think they meant to put me in here?" she asked.

"Maybe," he said. "Past here really is only the showers."

Ginny looked around. "It's definitely safer here. No temptation."

He led her to a door near the back of the room. "There's a closet. With some rearranging, we could probably fit some of your things in here." He unsnapped a key ring from his belt loop and unlocked the door.

Inside, the smell of worn leather, sweat, and dirt was overwhelming.

He coughed with a deep, choking laugh. "We'll need to air it out."

Deflated balls, a few out-of-service football shoulder pads, and a stack of sagging boxes covered the bottom. But with some shelves, yes, this could hold a lot more.

"This will be great," she said. "I can empty it out."

"I'll help," he said. "You want to come tomorrow afternoon, say two?" He jingled the keys. "I can get you in."

Her heart sped up a little. "Thank you," she said. "I'll definitely be here."

"Good. We can talk Roscoe strategy, among other things," he said. "See you then."

He strode back through the dressing room, his dress shoes ringing on the floor.

Ginny leaned against the door, her stomach fluttering. She would see him again tomorrow to clean a closet and discuss her dog.

Among other things.

CHAPTER 6

Carter pulled up behind the high school, looking for the green Jeep he'd seen parked at Ginny's rental house. She probably didn't know her way around, so he didn't want to go in without her.

The section of the school with the gym and dressing rooms was a large unbroken wall, only really discernible because it was taller than the rest. He couldn't assume she'd recognize it.

The lot was deserted, so he slowly circled, watching for her to drive up. As he made the next turn, he spotted her pulling up around front.

He rolled down his window. "Follow me to the back. There's a much closer door."

She wore a blue Eagles sweatshirt, the kind the booster club sold to raise money for the team. He liked that she was getting right into the spirit of the school, despite the fact that his team had lost thirty-five to nothing last night.

She'd been in the stands, sitting with a couple other teachers from the elementary school.

He parked his truck and jumped out. Ginny pulled up next to him, her ponytail swinging as she hopped out of her Jeep.

Ginny was different. Real different. Genuine. Focused. He liked that their time together was about other stuff, not just each other. Roscoe. Her job. Spending time with her was easy.

"Nice Jeep," he said. "A similar vintage to mine." He closed his door and locked it manually. The power locks had quit working years ago.

"Maybe they were in the car nursery together." She made a point of pushing down the lock on her car door, same as him.

They fell into step together. "I'm actually in the market for a new one," Carter said. "I just haven't been willing to let go of old Angel just yet."

"Angel?" Ginny squinted her eyes at him. "Let me guess. Mom? Aunt?"

He shook his head.

"Old girlfriend?" Her voice dripped with trepidation.

"They always ask that," Carter said with a laugh. "Angel was a cat we had when I was little. She was a stray, but I was convinced I could get her to live with us."

"Did she?"

"No. She broke my heart completely by running off with a tomcat after about six months. But I never forgot her. I had drawn literally fifty pictures of her."

"I have a story like that," Ginny said.

"You took in a stray cat who broke your heart?"

"No, actually, it was a rat."

They paused in front of the back door of the gym, and Carter extracted his keys. "A rat."

"Yes, I know. I think I watched Cinderella too many times. I had this notion that I could sew little jackets and hats for him."

"And how old were you?" He pushed the door open, and they walked inside. The interior was pitch black and smelled of gym socks and vinyl. Carter flipped on the lights.

"Nine, maybe?"

"So I'm guessing it didn't end well."

"Actually, my steady meals of cheese and bread kept him coming around for quite some time. Maybe two weeks."

"So did you ever get him dressed properly?"

Carter stopped walking, and they stood beneath one of the basketball hoops. It was nice seeing Ginny here in his space. She fit.

"Well, I made the clothes, and at one point, I managed to lure him into a box."

"All right, I'm hooked. I need the whole story." His words echoed in the big silent gym.

"He bit me. I ran straight to my mother. She took me to the hospital."

"Please tell me they didn't make you do rabies shots."

"No. I told them I had been feeding him for two weeks and that Herbert was a sweet rat, and they decided he probably wasn't rabid."

"Have you figured out since then that this doesn't happen unless they find the rat and test it?"

"Don't spoil my delusion!"

He grimaced, imagining how Ginny's dad mostly likely had dispatched of the rat that bit his little girl. "Okay, okay. Did you ever see Herbert again?"

"No. I kept his clothes for a long time, though."

They turned toward the boys' locker room, and he unlocked the outer door. "What are our childhoods for, except to traumatize us?"

She laughed. "I had a rather ordinary one. My only real beef was that they never let me have a dog."

They passed through the first door, and Carter flipped on the light. "Now you have a doozy."

The equipment room smelled mustier than yesterday, the scents all trapped overnight without the passage of students and the opening and closing of doors. Ginny wrinkled her nose, which made her look even more adorable. With her ponytail and Eagles sweatshirt, she could be one of the students.

They walked down the hall and into the dressing room. It was a good deal messier than when they had been there the day before, covered in wrappers, empty Gatorade bottles, a few scattered shirts, and an abandoned set of shoulder pads in the corner.

And dirt. Bits of caked mud were everywhere.

"Sorry about the mess," he said. "The cleaning staff won't come until very early Monday morning."

"Does the football team dress in here before the game?"

"No, my team knows better. The middle school team practiced on the field behind the school yesterday afternoon and changed here. I'll speak to their coach. They'll need to respect this space before they get on my team."

They approached the closet, and Carter unlocked the door.

"We can start pulling all the stuff out." He looked through the closet. "I don't think there will be much worth keeping."

He stepped inside the closet and began passing things to Ginny. She made stacks on the floor. Deflated sports balls. Old helmets. Parts and pieces of shoulder pads.

They opened the sagging boxes, discovering a pile of old jerseys.

"I don't even recognize the style," Carter said. "These might be from twenty or thirty years ago."

"What condition are they in?" she asked.

"The top ones, not so good," he said, pulling out the first one.

They dug through the box until they got four or five jerseys down. The top ones were dirty and stiff, unlikely to hold up to even a single washing.

But as they dug deeper, the red jerseys were still vivid and seemed protected from the elements by the layers of the others.

"Do you guys have any sort of faculty-student football game fundraiser type thing?" Ginny asked.

"Not since I've been here," he said. "But I know what you're talking about. At my high school, there would always be a volleyball match between the teachers and the team."

"I'm surprised you don't have anything like that here. Not for any of the sports?"

"Not in my two years. Maybe they did it in the past. What are you thinking?"

"Well, if the football team needed anything, shoes, meals, or whatever, a fundraiser game would be a way to use these jerseys."

He held one up. "That's definitely an idea. So we should hang on to them?"

"I think so. If nothing else, you should choose a good one and put it in the trophy case."

He dropped the jersey back in the box. "You're full of good ideas."

"It's because I'm a city girl," she said with a smile.

"Chicago, right?"

"For college. I was born in Seattle."

"You don't have much of an accent," he said.

"Probably because I took a lot of speech classes. I had trouble talking clearly early on. And a few other delays. It's a little bit of why I became a therapist myself."

He understood all that for sure. "The best kind of teacher is the one who's gone through the fire themselves."

Ginny separated the bad jerseys from the usable ones. "What about you? Why did you get into football coaching?"

"I played myself. Loved it. High school. College. I was supposed to be this hotshot. Supposed to get drafted high." He didn't meet her gaze, instead dragging out another box, heavy with cobwebs and dust. "I didn't get drafted at all. Had to scramble for a useful degree, anything I could use to get a job. Coaching was a natural fit."

He hated talking about this, so he started ripping tape off the next box, hoping she wouldn't ask for details.

She gathered up the strips of old tape. "Well, I'm glad you're here."

That was something, at least. "Thanks."

The last box held a surprise. Old vinyl signs, the sort you hang on the fence or at the bottom of stands in the stadium.

Ginny's face brightened. "Unroll one!"

He laid it out on the floor. It read *Applebottom Fishing Expeditions. Proud sponsors of the 1971 Eagles.*

"Wow," Ginny said. "It's older than we are!"

The next one read *Home of the Eagle State Champions.*

"So they used to be good?" she asked.

"A long time ago," Carter said. "There's trophies in the case."

"When did it go downhill?"

"Before we were born," he said.

He rolled up the sign and lifted another. *Applebottom Eagle Championship Years* was stenciled across the top with a series of dates. The last one was 1985.

"They had this one coach that led the team straight to the top," he said. "Couldn't have just been good players. The streak lasted, well," he tapped the range of dates, "fourteen years."

"The good players would graduate and go, but the team would still be good," Ginny said.

"Exactly. Anybody can win with a bunch of talent. It takes someone special to lead any collection of players to victory."

"You don't think that's you?" she asked.

He stuck the banner back in the box. "I couldn't lead myself to the starting roster at university. I doubt I'm going to take anybody to greatness."

Carter didn't mind Applebottom's losing tradition. He couldn't be blamed for it, and he didn't have to try to be something he wasn't.

Ginny ran her fingers along the banners, her eyes downcast. Probably she wasn't nearly so impressed

with him now that she knew he wasn't that interested in overachieving. And she probably didn't
know the half of it, although who knew what people
might have told her about him by now.

She spoke first. "Well, I don't need the whole
closet, so maybe we can combine these good jerseys
with this banner box to stay in there, and I'll use the
rest of the space."

His shoulders relaxed. She hadn't pushed.

Ginny moved the shirts from one box to another
while Carter left to carry the discards out to the
dumpster.

The metaphor wasn't lost on him. She'd hang on
to the good stuff, and he'd toss the trash.

CHAPTER 7

By the second week of school, Ginny was ready to start moving the kids into a curriculum that would hopefully advance their skills. She knew each of them by name. Seeing the reality of their abilities helped her prepare activities that would play up their strengths, so that they didn't feel frustrated, but would still be challenged.

On Tuesday morning, she realized that this was the day she and Carter would usually do a dog lesson. But they hadn't arranged anything after their closet clean out on Saturday, which had ended on a negative note. And she still didn't have his cell phone number.

Was he not interested in helping her with Roscoe after that hard talk? Had she been too nosy?

Maybe she could leave a message through the office, although that would certainly stir up gossip.

Still, their dog lessons were officially sanctioned by the Applebottom ladies. It wasn't like they didn't know. No one could sneeze in this town without someone holding out a box of tissue.

Ginny walked behind the secretary's desk and pulled her mail from the slot marked with her name. Inside was a small, handwritten note.

Ginny!

I don't think anyone has taught you to set up your voicemail. I have left you a couple of messages. I don't know your cell phone. Are we meeting Tuesday at our usual time and place? Here's my number.

Carter

Her face crept slowly with warmth as she ran her fingers over the numbers. So they were meeting again tonight, after all.

"Get something good?"

The voice so close to her shoulder startled her out of her skin.

It was Candace, a third-grade teacher. Two of her students were regulars in Ginny's room.

Ginny casually folded her stack of mail in half to hide the note from Carter.

"Just the usual. And a notice that I hadn't set up my voicemail for the district."

"Oh, that old thing," Candace said. She shook her head, sending her shiny black hair flowing like a shampoo commercial. She was one of those teachers who must have money separate from her salary. She dressed impeccably, with matching accessories and expensive shoes. Next to her, Ginny felt like a clod in her stretch pants with dirt on her knees.

"Mrs. Humphries at the front desk can help you," Candace said. "You want to do it pretty quick. A lot of parents like to use the system. You might have some messages stacked in there."

"Thanks. I'll ask her."

Ginny had shut off the ringer in her room because it might excite some of the kids who were easily startled. It didn't even occur to her that she would have voicemail.

Candace grabbed her stack of mail and headed out. The bell rang, and Ginny hurried toward her room. The voicemail would have to wait until the break. She needed to get to be ready for the students. And maybe take one more peek at the note from Carter.

When Carter stepped out of his truck, Ginny's Jeep was open, a leash trailing out of it to Roscoe, who sat just outside the door.

He paused on the sidewalk. Roscoe gave him a

doleful glance, then turned back to the interior of the back seat.

Ginny's voice came from inside. "Hop in, Roscoe. Come!" Her hand appeared, holding a bit of doggy bacon.

Roscoe leaned forward, trying to snag the bacon without actually stepping closer to the car.

"Roscoe!" Ginny's voice was impatient. "Get in this car! How will we ever go anywhere if you keep refusing?"

Carter stifled his laugh. Roscoe turned to him again, his eyes pleading to help him out.

"You're on your own," Carter said.

"Oh! Ouch!" Ginny's head smacked the door frame. "You're here!"

"I thought I'd walk with you to the park. Trying to get him to go in the car?"

Ginny emerged from the Jeep. Her pale blue jacket made her gray eyes shift to the color of an open sky. He felt sucker-punched.

"Every time he gets close to the car, he freezes up," she said, rubbing her head. "He must associate getting in with leaving someplace he loves."

"I'd balk, too."

Ginny stepped down and untangled her legs from the tether between her waist and Roscoe. She walked away from the car. Only when she closed the door did Roscoe leave his spot on the sidewalk, sniffing around to see if he could still get the bacon treat.

"I thought we were meeting on the hill," Ginny said.

"It's going to start getting dark earlier, so I might as well walk the lady both ways."

Ginny adjusted her backpack and fell into step beside him. Roscoe gave up on the treat and took the lead. Carter wrapped his arm around the leash between her waist and Roscoe, to give them some leverage if he took off.

They had gotten used to this arrangement last week, the closeness required due to the tether, and the step length necessary to match their strides. The knowledge was comfortable, like they had figured out some important part of each other. Roscoe quickly forgot his car lesson and dashed back and forth, sniffing and marking everything in their path.

"He's extra jumpy today, isn't he?" Carter asked.

"He is. Maybe it's because I've been pushing him lately. Trying to lure him into the car. Working on *sit* and *stay*."

"Could be. He also might sense the change in the seasons."

"He's a Chicago dog, so he may not know what to make of this extended warm spell," she said.

"Could be a storm coming. I checked the weather earlier, but it seemed like it wasn't going to happen until late at night."

"The sky doesn't look particularly ominous," she said.

"Maybe he just doesn't like Tuesdays," Carter said. "But I do." His body buzzed with an electric charge from admitting this to her. He'd been compelled to contact her when they parted on somber terms after their talk about the football team.

At first, when she didn't respond to his voice mails, he'd thought she didn't want to be seen with him again. But when her voice mail continued to have the generic district message, he'd realized she didn't know how to check it.

So he sent the note. Sometimes old-fashioned was good, even if the contents had most certainly been read by half of Applebottom. He could picture Sadie dropping it into the inner-district mail bag, scanning the contents and then relaying them to Betty and Delilah. He should have tracked down an envelope, but the message was simple enough.

Her eyes cut over at him, and his neck flushed hot.

Then abruptly she called out, "Roscoe! Way to ruin a moment!"

The dog was romantically urinating on a post.

They reached the walking path to the park. Roscoe dashed forward, and an entire flock of birds rose at once from the trees to settle farther away.

Roscoe leaped and barked, and Carter cinched a tighter hold on the leash. "Steady, boy."

"Roscoe!" Ginny called. "Sit!"

Roscoe stopped and turned to them with a question in the tilt of his head.

"Look that!" Carter exclaimed. "He knows we're talking to him!"

Ginny fumbled with her backpack. "Good boy, Roscoe!" She jerked out a packet of treats and opened them, but in her excitement she fumbled and dropped several on the ground.

Roscoe hustled back to gobble them up.

"You deserve them, Roscoe," Carter said, stroking his head.

Ginny glanced up at him, beaming. "He's getting it! Did you see how he stopped in his tracks? That should lead us into getting him to obey commands."

"We can definitely build on that." The enthusiasm in her voice made him smile. Ginny was good at living in the moment, forgetting her old disasters and reveling in the new. He should probably take a page from her playbook.

They walked on until they reached the spot where they had cut to the clearing last time. Roscoe knew the way and led them through the trees.

"My goal is to one day bring him here and take off his leash," Carter said.

"That's a crazy goal," Ginny said. "All I can picture is Roscoe tearing through the trees with us chasing after him."

"He's already doing better."

"Around you," she said.

They stood at the far ends of the tether, taking turns calling Roscoe's name. When he started actually moving between them, they added the word *come* after his name.

"This is going really well," Carter called out.

"A crazy improvement over last week!"

They tried *sit*, but Roscoe was too exuberant to actually sit at any point in the park.

"I think there are just too many distractions out here for him to settle in," Carter said.

Ginny agreed. "I'll keep working on him in my backyard. It's less exciting there."

A crack of thunder surprised them all. Ginny let out a little yelp, and Roscoe cowered to the ground.

"We better get back," Carter said.

Ginny tugged on Roscoe's leash and called his name, but he refused to move.

Carter bent down to place a hand on his back. "He's shaking like a leaf."

"I've never had him during a storm. I don't know what he's like."

Another peal of thunder cracked. Roscoe whined and turned to Carter, burying his head against Carter's belly.

"It's okay, boy," Carter said. "We're not going to let that big bad thunder get you."

Ginny moved toward the path out of the clearing and called out, "Roscoe." She held a treat.

Roscoe wouldn't budge.

"This might get interesting," she said.

Carter continued to stroke the dog. "Come on, boy. Let's go home." He stood up. Roscoe lifted his head, and Carter thought he might follow, but then lightning flashed and another roll of thunder rocked the clearing.

This time Roscoe jumped up and dashed for the trees.

Carter wasn't prepared to hold the tether, but Ginny started running the same direction to avoid to a sharp jerk on the harness around her waist.

Thankfully, Roscoe did not tear through the forest. As soon as he made it inside its protection, he stopped, frantically digging beneath a fallen log as if he could hide under it.

"Roscoe! Stop!" Ginny called. Dirt flew through the air, hitting her in the face, making it hard to approach him.

Carter circled the flying dirt to the other side of the log.

"Roscoe," he said softly, leaning in, "you're okay. It's okay."

Roscoe paid him no mind. He continued digging as fast as his paws would go. The dirt beneath the log was damp and soon he flung mud in every direction. Ginny stood behind him, her hands to her face. The tether was too short for her to back away from the flying clods of dirt.

"Come over to this side," Carter said.

She hopped over the log, settling in next to him. Roscoe frantically continued to dig.

"What do we do?" she asked.

"Pray that the thunder stops so he'll calm down?"

Roscoe dug as if his life depended on it. Carter had no idea how to make him stop.

"I've seen this behavior in children, many times," Ginny said. "The urge to hide when they're afraid led me to keep a pile of blankets in a corner so they could cover up until they were in control again."

"It works?"

"Sure. In some of the homes I serviced before, scary people coming in and out would create this behavior. Maybe Roscoe's been through something."

"What would you do if Roscoe was one of your kids?" he asked.

"Cover him. That way he'd feel sheltered."

"Then let's do it," Carter said. "You still have that picnic blanket?"

"I do." Ginny turned her backpack around and grabbed the roll. She snapped it out so that it floated over Roscoe, eventually settling down on his frantic body.

His digging slowed down as the blanket covered him.

"Roscoe," she said softly. "Roscoe, Roscoe, Roscoe." She sang his name as if it were a lullaby.

Carter watched in amazement as Roscoe stopped digging. He dropped to his belly, panting from the effort, only his nose sticking out from the blanket.

"You did it," Carter whispered, struck with awe. "You tamed the beast."

Ginny kept crooning to Roscoe as they carefully climbed over the log to his side. Carter hoped the thunder wouldn't return, not at this critical moment.

A soft pattering of raindrops hit the canopy of leaves above them. He glanced over at Ginny in concern.

"Hopefully the rain will stay easy," she said quietly.

They were somewhat protected. Only the occasional fall of water from a heavy leaf caused a gentle cascade through the trees. They knelt on either side of Roscoe, petting his head.

After a little while, Ginny slowly peeled the blanket back, calling his name softly in a singsong voice.

When the blanket was off and rolled back up, they managed to lift Roscoe to standing. The three of them walked slowly and carefully through the damp woods, listening to the rain.

"When we reach the edge of the trees," Ginny asked, "Should we just walk home?"

Carter pulled out his phone to check the weather. "This is a pretty small cloudburst according to the radar," he said. "I say we sit here and wait it out."

And they did, finding another fallen log at the

treeline looking over the park. The rain fell softly on the lake as the muted gray-tinged sunset hit the water beyond the cloudburst.

The world was foggy and damp and smelled earthy and full of life. Roscoe sat between them, his nose in the air, sniffing at the fresh smells. All the animals in the woods were tucked away, so there was nothing to excite him.

Neither of them spoke. They simply took in the glorious park, the end of summer, and the way the three of them had worked together so perfectly to avert disaster.

CHAPTER 8

The week passed more quickly than Ginny expected. She and Carter met for another Tuesday and found a bit of success when Roscoe finally connected the word *sit* with putting his bottom down on the ground.

She was sure the other parkgoers in Applebottom that day got a good laugh at watching the football coach and the occupational therapist run all over the hill, stopping to shout, "Roscoe, sit!" every few feet, then giggle like maniacs when the dog did what most dogs could already do.

They hadn't made any progress on *stay* yet, but Ginny had hope. Progress was progress. For now, they limited their adventures to the park or quiet neighborhoods far from anyone who had seen his rampage through Town Square a few weeks ago.

Every other football game was a home game, so

on the Friday after their success, Ginny headed back to the bleachers. This time, Carly showed up with her baby and husband. And Natalie, one of the fourth-grade teachers Ginny worked with, also sat near them in the faculty and student section of the stadium.

Ginny took care not to stare at Carter as much as she might have if she were alone. The women seemed pretty intuitive, and Ginny wasn't prepared to out anything that was happening—or maybe *not* happening—between her and Carter so early on.

They cheered whenever the Eagles had the ball, and winced every time the other team scored, which was a lot. Ginny remembered Carter's goal of scoring fourteen points in a season and realized it really *was* a challenge. Everyone stood up when the Eagles kicker got a chance at a field goal.

He missed.

Carly's baby got fussy after halftime, so they took off. Ginny remained with Natalie, determined to sit out the game even though a cold front had blown in and the air cooled rapidly.

"I wonder if our football team should just be disbanded," Natalie said. "I've been teaching here six years, and I don't think we've ever won a game."

Ginny's heart clenched at the thought of Carter being sent away. "Didn't one of the students get a football scholarship last year?" she asked. A boy named Caden who used to play for the Eagles had spoken at the pep rally.

"Sure," Natalie said. "But right now, we're an embarrassment."

"I found some banners about all the years in a row that we won championship titles."

Natalie tilted her head. "Where did you find those?"

"In a closet I'm using at the high school." Ginny didn't have to admit that she found them *with* the current football coach.

A pair of little old ladies passed in front of them on the bleachers, spotted Ginny, and put their heads together to whisper.

What was that about?

She leaned in to Natalie so her voice wouldn't carry. "Who are they?"

"Oh, that's Gertrude and Maude. They own a pie shop on Town Square. Amazing pies. You should totally go in there."

"Do you think they're talking about me?"

"No doubt. Gertrude and Maude are all up in everybody's business in Applebottom."

"Should I worry about this?"

Natalie laughed. "I wouldn't. They're harmless."

"Which one is which?"

"Maude is the friendly one," Natalie said. "Gertrude looks like she's just bit a lemon."

Ginny bit back a smile. Gertrude, with her helmet

of white hair and sour expression, did indeed seem to be permanently displeased.

She tried to force her attention back on the game, then realized she was staring at Carter, and certainly those women would notice. They climbed a couple steps to be level with Ginny and Natalie, then made their way down the row.

They were coming to sit next to them!

Ginny took a deep breath, trying to be calm. Probably they were just coming to inquire about how Roscoe's training was going. Maybe they were doing some sort of risk assessment about her ability to take the dog anywhere near their pie shop.

"Miss Ginny," Gertrude said. "Look at you, all full of pointless Eagle spirit."

Ginny tugged self-consciously at her sweatshirt. "Hello."

Maude leaned forward, her tight black curls and grandmotherly air making her much easier to smile at. "Don't mind Gertie," Maude said. "She wouldn't know Eagle spirit if it bit her in the tush." She extended a hand. "I'm Maude."

"Nice to meet you," Ginny said. She hoped she sounded more confident than she felt.

Maude elbowed her friend. "Well, introduce yourself, Gertie. You got the poor girl all nervous."

Nope. They knew.

"A little fear will do her good," Gertrude said. "This generation has no respect for their elders."

Maude elbowed her again, and Gertrude sighed. "The name's Gertrude, not Gertie. I put salt on that woman's pie for calling me that on the regular. We're friends with Delilah."

Great. So they knew about Roscoe's disaster.

Maude peered around Gertrude. "Did you get the book she sent?"

"I did," Ginny said. "Carter's been helping me train Roscoe. It takes both of us sometimes to get him in line."

Maude bumped Gertrude on the arm. "I knew he'd be the perfect thing," she said. "Didn't I tell you he would be the perfect thing?"

Gertrude pinched her lips. She looked perturbed that Maude would take credit. "I believe it was Topher who suggested the football coach. Not you."

Maude shrugged. "Well, it's working." She leaned forward again. "I do hope you'll come to our pie shop soon. I'd love to sit and chat a spell."

"We might as well talk now," Gertrude said, gesturing at the field. "It's not like this team is going to score any points."

But, as if the world wanted to prove her wrong, a roar rose up from the Eagle side of the stands. The quarterback decided not to throw the ball and tucked it under his arm to take off running.

"First down, Eagles!" The announcer shouted over the loudspeaker. He sounded surprised.

"I don't think they're doing too bad," Ginny said.

"But I would be delighted to come by your shop. I can leave Roscoe at home."

Maude beamed, her dark cheeks turning rosy in the stadium light. Ginny definitely liked her over Gertrude.

"That will be just perfect."

"That would be *necessary*," Gertrude added. "We can't have your dog eating an entire day's profits."

"Gertrude is not a dog lover," Maude said. "But she has other good qualities."

"I bet you can't name two," Gertrude said.

"You make good pies," Maude said.

Gertrude folded her hands in her lap. "Well, I'll give you that."

Since nobody offered up a second good quality for Gertrude, Ginny tried to watch the game. The quarterback attempted a couple more throws, but nobody was open to receive them. On fourth down, he decided to keep it again, and got another first down on his own.

Despite the women being so close, and no doubt with eagle eyes, Ginny snuck a peek at Carter. A good coach recognized when he had an opportunity. She assumed he would let the quarterback keep holding onto the ball. It was the only way the team was getting any headway.

But no, for the next several downs, the quarterback shunted the ground play to other carriers who were instantly tackled, or tossed the ball to receivers who couldn't break free to get a clear catch.

Despite the quarterback's gains, they ended up punting.

Ginny wondered why Carter wasn't continuing what was clearly working. Was he worried about the quarterback getting hurt?

She knew a fair amount about football. Her father was a huge Seahawks fan, and they spent a lot of Sundays dissecting the coach's calls. A quarterback keeper was a powerful play if a team had someone who could do it well.

She would ask Carter about it. Surely he had his reasons. At the end of the third quarter, Gertrude and Maude complained about the cold and left. A lot of the stands had emptied out. The Eagles were losing fifty-four to nothing.

Natalie didn't want to ditch her alone, but Ginny told her it was fine if she was done. Ginny wanted to see if the quarterback would get any more yards on his own.

"No, I'll stay," Natalie said. "I want to hear about what you've been doing with the football coach. Every unattached girl in Applebottom tried to catch his eye when he got here," she said. "Nothing ever got past the third date. Not so much as a kiss. I don't know what he's looking for, but we were not it."

"Did you go out with him?" Ginny was a little afraid of the answer.

"No, he never asked me. Not for my lack of trying. But I'm at the elementary school, and he's over at the high school. We didn't cross paths a whole lot."

Ginny wondered if that meant she thought she still had an opportunity.

Natalie went on. "Julia Hampton, the French teacher, did manage to snog him. But she was drunk on frozen margaritas and forced herself on him at the faculty retreat last summer. It didn't go well for her."

Ginny followed Carter as he walked along the sideline. She shouldn't ask questions, but the way Carter had left things after they cleaned the closet made her painfully curious.

"How so?"

"He wouldn't even talk to her after that. I don't know, maybe there's something wrong with him. He's been three and out with every girl. He got jilted in college pretty publicly. Nobody really blames him for being gun shy."

"What happened?"

Natalie raised her eyebrows. "You have to tell me what's up first."

Ginny shrugged. "I have hung out with him a little."

"Tell me everything."

"I thought everybody knew," she said. "The owner of the dog bakery forced him to come help me with my dog. Roscoe is too big for me to control, and I'm trying to train him."

Natalie deflated a little. "Oh. Yeah. Carter is always taking on projects like that. You can absolutely ask him to help clean out your garage, or plant some trees, or haul a load out to the dump. But if you want to get up close, it's just not gonna happen."

"So about that public jilting?"

Natalie's eyes flashed. She was a natural gossip. "Carter was seeing this girl in college. You know the type. Perfect, pretty, rich. She had her eyes set on him because she thought he would go pro in football."

"He didn't get drafted," Ginny said.

"Exactly," Natalie said. "She dropped him like a hot potato. Carter had set up this marriage proposal thing on camera. When she realized he wasn't signing, she gave a little huff and took off. It made a bunch of the sports news shows. You can probably find it on YouTube."

"That's pretty terrible." Ginny hadn't thought to search for Carter online. Maybe she should. "He must've really cared her about to propose."

"Who knows," Natalie said. "She looked like a gold digger to me. But maybe he couldn't see it."

"He seems like a nice guy," she said.

Natalie nudged Ginny with her shoulder. "So there *is* something there. Well, good luck with that. Maybe this dog thing will be exactly what you need to get up close and personal."

The last seconds of the clock ran down, and the teams met on the field. The stands were virtually empty. The band played a song, and the cheerleaders, considerably less energetic than they had been at the beginning, shook their pom-poms.

Ginny watched Carter shake hands with the other team's coach. The band struck up the school song, and he turned to face them, his hat over his heart.

And that's when he spotted her. Their eyes locked. Ginny gave him a little salute and a thumbs up.

He returned her greeting with a slow smile.

"I saw that," Natalie said. "If there were a leaderboard for the Applebottom football coach, you'd be right at the top."

CHAPTER 9

On the Monday morning after the football game, Ginny found another handwritten note in her faculty mailbox.

Mrs. Humphries, the secretary, gave Ginny a sly nod as she passed. Clearly, she knew about the note.

The first half-hour of the school day was always quiet as the teachers settled their students before moving any of them down to occupational therapy. Ginny sat on one of the bouncy balls and pulled out the note.

Ginny,

I know we exchanged numbers, but I sort of like being old-fashioned. Thank you for staying at the football game all the way to the bitter end. It mattered to me. You've earned your Eagle wings.

I've been thinking about that Titanic Museum you mentioned. I haven't been in a long time, and I would be happy to take you. Perhaps this weekend? It's not too crowded if we go in the late afternoon, after the tourists leave. Let me know.

Carter

Ginny wanted to let out a huge squeal, but at that moment, her door opened and an aide brought in the first visitor for the day—Caleb, a second grader with balance problems.

Ginny quickly thrust her mail into a drawer and called him over. They walked the balance path and practiced crossing his midline to help his brain pass a motion from one hemisphere to the other.

But even as Ginny worked with Caleb, correcting him and praising what he did well, the back of her mind stayed on Carter. He had asked her to go to the museum. Was it an actual date? Or more of a friend-zone thing? Would she only get three chances like Natalie said? And if that were true, should she hold off? If they got to the three dates, and he tried to throw her over, did that mean that the dog lessons would end also?

"Miss Ginny?" Caleb tugged on her shirt.

"I'm sorry, Caleb. My brain was somewhere else."

Caleb laughed. "How did it get out of your head?"

"I don't know. Let's go catch it."

They ran over to the circle of uneven padded mats, pretending to snatch her brain. Caleb almost fell a couple times, but Ginny was there to catch him and right him again. He had already made progress since the beginning of the school year.

As long as they worked with him as he grew, he would master this balance problem over time.

At the end of his twenty minutes, Ginny escorted him back to class.

When she returned, she quickly pulled out the note and read it one more time. What should she do? Accept the offer and worry that her clock was ticking? Or turn him down, which might mean they would never progress past simply training her dog?

How much stock should she put in what Natalie had told her at the game?

She needed advice.

During her short lunch break, Ginny sought Carly, who sat at her desk, twisting her blond hair into a high bun.

"Coming to lunch?" Ginny asked. "Maybe we could sit outside today?"

Carly surveyed the leaves blowing past her window. "Are you looking for some privacy for girl talk?" She opened one of her drawers and pulled out her lunch box. "Because I'm totally game. But maybe we could stay in here? You realize we're in the middle of a cold spell."

"Yes, I was trying to avoid the faculty lounge."

"I have to be quick today," Carly said. "Lisa has a substitute, so I'm watching some of her kids to reduce the load on the sub."

Ginny sat in a student chair at a nearby table and opened her lunch. "You can't tell anyone, okay?"

Carly moved to sit opposite her. They squatted on the little chairs like giants. "Mum's the word."

Ginny's words came in a rush. "Natalie told me at the football game on Friday that Carter has gone three strikes and out with everyone he's dated."

"I'm not sure that's completely accurate," Carly said. "But I wasn't on the market, so I may not know the gritty details."

"Okay, well, the thing is, he asked me to go to the Titanic Museum. I can't tell if it's like a date-date, or like a friend-date, because I mentioned that I really wanted to go there."

Carly aimed her sandwich at Ginny. "That's totally a date-date."

"Are you sure? Because everything we've done together has been very friend-like. So I could see him just saying hey, let's go to this museum."

Carly shook her head. "No way. The Titanic Museum is romantic. There's a giant staircase. The story of Jack and Rose. The tragic ending."

"That's what I'm trying to avoid!"

Carly laughed. "Ginny, it will be fine. If it's three dates and out, then that just means it wasn't meant to be."

"But I would hate to lose his help with my dog."

Carly got thoughtful, tugging the top crust of her sandwich. "That's true. If you guys burn out on the dates, then you don't get to see him at all."

"See? Does it make more sense for me to try to keep the dog thing going, and maybe he'll get more comfortable with me? Maybe then we could avoid the three and out."

"I'm still not confident that it's a three-and-out situation. And you have to consider what message it sends him if you turn him down."

Ginny stuck her half-eaten sandwich back in its container. "I wish there was some way I could say no without actually saying no."

"Women have been doing that for ages," Carly said. "I have to wash my hair. I'm on my period." She laughed. "Don't say that."

"I guess I could just be busy and maybe put it off. That way I could say yes, but not do it yet. Buy me some time."

"That seems like a viable strategy." Carly glanced up at the clock. "Oh crap, I have to go. She shoved the rest of her sandwich in her mouth and put her box back in the drawer. "I guess this is good for the diet," she said around the mound of bread. "Nice chat. Tell me how it goes."

Ginny picked up her own lunch to take back to her room. She knew what to do now. Hopefully, as she bought more time, she and Carter could figure out if they were indeed compatible without having to go through the third and possibly final date to find out.

CHAPTER 10

Ginny stayed after school that day to put together a handwritten note, just like the one Carter had sent. This method was possibly too romantic for what she had to say, but in many ways, it was also a safer bet. With a note left in a slot, they wouldn't start a back-and-forth conversation that could trip her up as she tried to delay the date.

She balled up three or four versions before finally coming up with one. She told him that going to the museum was an amazing idea, and she really looked forward to it. But could they postpone? She had a crazy weekend ahead, and she wanted to really take the time that they would need to see a museum of that magnitude.

Hopefully that would work.

Just in case there were prying eyes, Ginny folded

the paper up and sealed it in an envelope. She wrote *Carter McBride* on the outside in a plain simple script so that there would be no funny ideas that this might be a love note.

Truly, it *wasn't*. Technically Ginny was turning him down.

By the time she finished, most of the staff was gone, and Ginny realized she would need to drive the note over to the high school in order to make sure he got it before they saw each other at the park the next day.

By the time she walked home, let Roscoe out for a little while, and prepared to drive up to the high school, it was well after five. Since the high school let out at four, there was a real risk that she wouldn't be able to get into the building at all. She decided to go early the next morning instead.

As the evening wound down, Ginny almost gave in to the temptation to send Carter a quick text message. But the fear that he might immediately ask *what's happening next weekend* held her back. She didn't want to lie.

Ginny started her day extra early to drive by the high school before the elementary bell. She was through the front door and in the office before she realized she had no clue where the teacher boxes were at the high school. When she arrived on Fridays, she always went straight to the gym.

The high school started an hour later than the

elementary, so the rooms were silent and empty. Ginny wandered the administrative wing, glancing around. She passed offices for the assistant principal and the counselor, and two copy machines.

Then she found it—a small space with rows of cubbies.

Names were stickered below each one. They were not alphabetical, but seemed to be arranged by subject matter. After a moment, Ginny found the cluster for the coaches, and spotted Carter's name.

The turn of her heart upon seeing it made clear that she was feeling more attached to him than she had admitted. But after getting caught touching his nameplate in the athletic offices, Ginny didn't risk stroking this one and embarrassing herself.

She stuck the envelope in his cubby and turned around, almost crashing into a man in a tweed jacket.

"Oh!" she said. "I'm so sorry!"

"Not a problem," the man replied. He was older, but not terribly so—probably late thirties. He had a friendly expression and crystal blue eyes.

"Who are you?" he asked.

"I'm the occupational therapist. I work here on Fridays."

Ginny desperately wanted to escape, fearing this man would figure out what she had done. The cubbies were mostly empty, and she felt as though the lone envelope sticking out of Carter's box was flashing like a neon sign.

"I'm Andrew McCallister," he said, holding out a hand. "History teacher."

Ginny shook it awkwardly. Andrew was dressed like a stuffy 1950s professor, with his tweedy brown jacket and bow tie. She vaguely remembered someone talking about him in connection to some secret messages on the cakes you could buy on Town Square. Not that Ginny had bought one. She avoided Town Square completely.

"Nice to meet you," Ginny said. "I've got a race back over to the elementary school to start my day."

"Have a good one." His eyes scanned the boxes, and once again Ginny worried that the single envelope in Carter's cubby stood out. It was probably just her. There were loose papers in some of the other slots.

Maybe this romantic plan of handwritten notes wasn't such a great idea after all.

She resisted the urge to pluck it out and left the office.

By lunchtime, Ginny regretted her decision to write a note. Had he seen it yet? Did he think she was making excuses?

Ginny was so distracted, it was hard to focus on the students. She kept picturing Carter at his mail slot—his brown hair, that chiseled face, his strong shoulders in a school sweatshirt. She had to work diligently to make sure she gave her full attention to the students.

It didn't help that it was a lighter day than usual, as one entire grade had gone to a field trip, leaving gaps of empty time for her to obsess.

Of course, there was always the possibility that he wouldn't even get the note before they met for the dog lesson tonight. If he'd already checked his box early that morning, he might not look again until tomorrow.

Ginny would think of that *now*.

"I really am just a teenage girl at heart," she muttered as she rearranged the stability balls in their perfect circle.

"What was that, dear?"

Ginny turned to the door, her stomach flipping from the surprise. The school secretary, Mrs. Humphries, stood there holding a folder.

"Just talking to myself," she said. "Can I help you?"

"You're getting a new student tomorrow. New to the district. He'll be in third grade. The coordinator thought you should review this before you saw him the first time. The teacher wasn't sure when she would bring him by."

Ginny walked across the room and took the folder from her. "Thank you," she said. "I'll be sure to go over it before tomorrow."

Mrs. Humphries glanced around the room. "I love what you've done in here. It looks amazing."

"It's going well," she said.

"Enough to make you feel like a teenage girl?"

Ginny's face burned. "Something like that," she said.

Mrs. Humphries raised her eyebrows, as if she knew that her work had nothing to do with her mutterings.

Small town life. On days like this, Ginny sort of wished she'd moved someplace as big as Chicago.

CHAPTER 11

Carter parked his truck in front of Ginny's house just before five o'clock. Her note to him sat on the passenger seat. He killed the engine and picked it up with a frown.

He didn't know what to make of it. She had been so fired up to see the Titanic Museum, but this note felt a lot like a brush off.

Maybe she wasn't feeling it.

He shoved the note in the glove compartment and got out of the truck. He'd get a feel from her tonight, one way or the other. If she wasn't interested, then that was that. He definitely wouldn't press.

He rapped on her door. Through the wall, he could hear Roscoe's excited bark, and Ginny trying to subdue him.

When they appeared, Roscoe lunged forward, only half harnessed.

"I'm sorry. I'm running a little late," she said.

Carter firmly grasped the dog's collar. "Somebody's ready for a walk, aren't you, Roscoe?" He tried to steal a glance at Ginny, but she was in the middle of frantically strapping her harness to her waist, and he couldn't see her expression.

"Come in while I finish this," she said.

Carter stepped into her house. Everything was neat and tidy, other than the scattered dog supplies next to her backpack on the floor. When the door was safely closed, Carter let go of the collar.

Roscoe leaped up and placed his paws on Carter's shoulders. This had become their regular greeting. Carter accepted a couple licks and then set him on the ground.

"Roscoe, *sit*," he said.

Roscoe attempted another leap up to Carter's shoulders.

"Yeah, it's sort of two steps forward, one step back," Ginny said. "He hasn't sat once today."

"Interesting," Carter said. "He was doing it so well last week."

"I know. And he did yesterday. But today it's like his memory has been erased."

"I'm sure dogs get in moods just like the rest of us."

Ginny fastened the harness around her waist, cinching the sides for a snug fit. On someone small like Ginny, it had a corset affect, drawing her waist into tiny proportions.

His jaw tightened, and he glanced away. Probably she wasn't even interested in him, so he needed to quit ogling her. He focused on Roscoe as she slipped her jacket on top of the entire ensemble and held out the loose end of the leash.

"You want to do the honors?" she asked. Her face was flushed from the effort of getting everything together quickly.

Or maybe she'd caught him looking.

Carter took the leash, and their fingers brushed against each other. He forced himself not to react, even though everything in him had flared hot. Sparks practically flew from where they touched, and their eyes held for a moment.

Maybe it was time to address this. "I got your note," he said.

Her lips parted as she let out a breath. "We'll do it soon, right?"

Okay, that seemed like interest. Maybe she really did have something to do. "Yeah," he said.

She relaxed, so he knew this was the right course. Bring it down. No pressure.

He broke their gaze and attached the leash to Roscoe's harness.

Carter cleared his throat. "At least the weather looks fine today. A little cold is all." He was dressed for it in jeans and a sweatshirt.

"Then hopefully we won't be trying to calm a dog in the rain and muck!" she said.

"That was a memorable day, for sure."

Their gazes clashed, and Carter figured she was thinking about that moment in the trees where they looked out over the park. They stood there too long, and Roscoe gave an impatient *woof*.

Ginny looked down. "Okay, Roscoe! We're going!"

The spell was broken, and they left the house, heading down the street in their usual easy-going manner.

When they arrived at the hill, they returned to their standby commands, getting Roscoe's attention, and convincing him to sit. At first, he didn't oblige, but then Ginny brought out the treat bag. Light dawned on both of them as Roscoe started sitting immediately when he recognized a reward was involved.

"He's figured it out," Carter said. "He expects that treat."

"The book said not to worry about that," Ginny said. "It's a natural part of it. And actually pretty helpful, because once he figures out he gets these rewards for doing what we want, he will do more."

"Okay," Carter said. "Should we work on *stay*?"

"I don't think he's up for *stay*. I would be happy with *come*. If I can get him to come when I call him, then I don't have to worry about him going into one of the businesses downtown if he's not supposed to."

"Sounds good to me."

Ginny reached for the connection to her harness to release Roscoe.

"I'll give us some room to see if Roscoe will come to me," she said.

"Sounds good."

Ginny pulled on the release, but it was twisted in a strange position. She couldn't get it loose. "Can you get this?" she asked.

"Sure." He moved in close, his hands near her waist.

Ginny smelled of pine needles and something feminine, like a flower shampoo. Carter had to swallow over a lump in his throat at their proximity.

His fingers fumbled a moment, then finally the tether came loose. "You were right. It was good and stuck."

"It really wasn't an excuse to get you close."

The tone in her voice made him grin. When Ginny lifted her face, their mouths were only inches apart. They stared at each other for another long beat, and Carter spotted little specs of gold in her brown eyes.

For a long moment they held the position. Only the smallest movement would have brought them together.

Carter's arm jerked back suddenly. Roscoe had taken off after a bird. "I need to stay on top of this,"

Carter said, dashing to catch up. "He almost got away."

Carter let Roscoe get a few paces up the hill, then firmly told him to *sit*. When Roscoe spotted the treat in Carter's hand, he did.

"He's looking for it," Carter called back. "He's figuring it out."

Ginny bent down and slapped her hands on her knees. "Roscoe, *come*."

Roscoe looked at her hands. She reached for the backpack, and Roscoe already knew what she was going for. He bounded her direction.

Ginny fed him the treat. "I'm not sure he's getting the connection between the word and coming to me."

"I agree," Carter said. "Let me fetch a couple treats, and we'll go back and forth."

They did that for a good half hour, still not sure that Roscoe wasn't coming for the treat instead of the word. As they walked back home, Ginny said, "Maybe I need to get some sort of little treat sack that is always fastened to me. That way we know for sure he's coming because we say the word, not because we've already put a treat in our hands."

"Good thinking," Carter said. "I'm headed into Branson on Saturday. You want me to pick one up at the pet store? They have a lot more options than here."

"That would be great," she said.

"Since you have such a crazy weekend and all," he added.

Only when her pace faltered did he realize what that sounded like, as if he was accusing her of making up an excuse not to go to the museum.

The silence stretched between them, and Carter felt obligated to fill it. "I bet you still have boxes that are packed."

Ginny fumbled with the treat bag to avoid looking him in the eye. "I do want to go," she said. "Just not yet."

"It's fine."

They walked on, Roscoe dashing from one side of the street to the other, testing the limits of his tether. He was a good distraction in the awkwardness.

Carter wasn't one for games. Not usually. But he really liked Ginny. Maybe she had more problems than it seemed. He was the one who felt gun shy after his big miss on national television.

She was new in town. Nobody knew her past. Possibly she had some experience that was just as humiliating as his.

CHAPTER 12

The Friday football schedule showed an away game, but it was in a neighboring town, so Ginny called Natalie and the two of them drove over the bridge to watch it anyway.

Once again, the quarterback kept the ball when he couldn't find an opening and made quick progress up the field. But just like before, Carter instructed him to keep passing or running ground plays rather than actually helping the team toward its modest goal of fourteen points in a season. Strange.

Carter spotted Ginny early on, as the visitor's side was almost empty other than the band and cheer-leaders, plus the football parents. Several times she caught him glancing up at her.

Natalie did too. "I saw that," she said. "He ask you out yet?"

Ginny didn't want to admit that he had. "We're

still doing the dog lessons," she said. "But maybe it will be in the cards."

"Three and out, I'm telling you."

Ginny had no answer to that.

When the game ended, Natalie grabbed Ginny's hand and dragged her to the break in the chain-link fence where the team walked to go to the dressing rooms.

As Carter passed, Natalie called out, "Hey, Coach!"

Ginny's stomach roiled. What was she doing?

But Carter ambled over, waving to the few Eagle fans who had paused to let the team pass before heading to their cars.

"Hey, Ginny. Thanks for coming." He looked quizzically at Natalie. "I think we've met before."

"I'm at the elementary with Ginny," Natalie said. She grinned and looked from Carter to Ginny, as if she could glean something. "I hear you two have been seeing each other a lot."

"Just for the dog," Ginny said quickly.

"Roscoe is great," Carter said.

"Maybe you should do something without Roscoe," Natalie said.

Ginny's body burst hot with shock. "Natalie!"

Carter seemed less surprised, waving at another couple walking by. "Maybe so. I should head in with the boys."

"Yeah, great seeing you!" Natalie said.

When he turned away, Ginny had to control herself to avoid exploding. Keeping her voice measured and calm, she asked, "Why did you do that?"

"Just a little friendly suggestion for our hot coach!" she said. "Come on. You're into him!"

Ginny tightened her jacket around her body. Her friendship with Carter wasn't possible to hide in a town this small. And it seemed everyone was trying to push them together maybe a little faster than they wanted to do it themselves.

A coach's meeting made Carter run late the next Tuesday. He texted Ginny to let her know he'd meet her at the park, and he had the new treat bag.

The meeting had not gone well. Parents were calling in about the major losses with unanswered points. Several people asked why they weren't using the new quarterback more effectively.

He was on edge and worked hard to bring himself down before he met up with Ginny.

When he finally managed to make it to their hill, he spotted Ginny and her dog looking over Table Rock Lake. The sun was already low in the sky, spilling red light across the water and leaving them in silhouette.

They looked perfect and serene, the ideal thing to take away the ugliness of his day.

He paused for a moment, wondering if he should broach the topic of the museum again, or if he ought to wait for her to come around. Maybe she wasn't interested, but then, after that moment with Roscoe in the storm, they had some connection, something he'd never quite felt before.

And her friend had been pushy after the game. Had Ginny told her about him? Ginny had been upset at the interference, but maybe only because it caught her by surprise?

Ginny spotted him and waved. They bounded down the hill, Roscoe leading the way. The Great Dane leapt up and put his paws on Carter's shoulders. This was becoming one of his favorite things about the dog.

"Roscoe!" Ginny called. "Down! Sit!"

The dog ignored her, shoving his nose in Carter's face. He laughed. "Here," he said, tossing the new treat bag around the big brute for Ginny to catch.

She looked it over. "It's perfect!" She attached it to her belt and slid a few bacon chews inside while Carter wrangled Roscoe back to the ground.

When his paws hit the grass, his snout lifted into the air.

"I think he's noticed," Carter said.

Roscoe hustled back to Ginny, poking his nose to her belly and sniffing at the new bag.

"I'll hold on to him," Carter said. "Walk a little ways and show him your empty hands."

Roscoe didn't want to let Ginny and her tantalizing smell go. Carter held on tightly to his harness as Ginny tried to walk.

She held up her empty hands. "I don't have anything, Roscoe," she said.

Roscoe strained against the leash. Carter had to dig in his heels to hold him back. "We created a monster," he said.

"I know. I don't really know what to do about it."

"Maybe we should just walk for a while and try to let him forget where they are."

That was wishful thinking. Even as they moved along the path, Roscoe constantly nudged the treat bag at Ginny's waist.

"We may have to scuttle this for another day," Ginny said. "Maybe if I put the treats in when he's not around, the smell of them won't be so obvious. I can wash my hands and everything."

Carter nodded. "I see why people need trainers. The books and YouTube videos talk generically about dogs, but you need someone to help you adjust your strategy on the fly."

"He walks right beside us as long as the treat bag is attached to me," Ginny said. "I would call that a win."

It was true. This was the most pleasant walk they'd ever had with her dog.

"At least it's good for something," Carter said.

The sun tipped the edge of the lake, so they made their way back to Ginny's house.

"It was nice of you to drive out to the game Friday," he said. "I liked seeing you there."

Her face pinked up a little. This was working. He had been right to ask her out. But why had she delayed?

"It's fun. Like all the times watching football with my dad."

"Really? You guys did that?" Most girls he met weren't too into sports.

"We would have great arguments about strategy," she said.

He grinned at her. "My dad was a big fan, too. Who did you root for?"

"Seattle," she said.

"Bummer," he teased. "And just when I was starting to like you."

She laughed. "High school is more interesting, since the talent really stands out. You were right about that quarterback being so good. When he keeps the ball, you guys actually make some progress."

This sounded a lot like what he heard at the meeting. He hadn't expected it from Ginny. "Toby's got talent. Too bad he's stuck with us."

Ginny plunged on. "But if he's got promise, he should be allowed to do what he does well and get the statistics that might help with college and scholarship."

Carter's defenses flared. "For what? To be disappointed when he gets benched because he came from nowhere important? When nobody drafts him?"

Ginny let out a long gust of air. "Whoa-kay," she said. "You're the coach. You know best."

Carter forced himself to relax. She was just trying to be helpful. She couldn't know what he was saddled with. "No, I'm sorry. I shouldn't snap at you. I just don't want him to get his hopes up. It's easy to look good on a team like ours."

The fallen leaves crunched beneath their feet in the quiet. Most of Applebottom seemed to be in for the night, the blue glow of televisions showing through the windows, and the aroma of home-cooked meals coming from kitchens.

Roscoe sniffed the air, and for the first time in the walk, forgot about the treat bag and tried to aim for one of the doors.

"Looks like Roscoe finally found something more tantalizing than the treats," Ginny said.

The change of topic was more than welcome. Carter looked down at the dog. "Even so, he's still not pulling like he was. It's good progress."

It was true. Roscoe moved at the end of his tether, but he was still walking along at the same rate as they were.

"I guess I can hope that my days of being dragged

from one side of the street to the other are over," Ginny said.

"He's doing great. He sits. He comes when you call. He's actually walking with us."

His gut slowly unclenched now that they were talking normally again.

"Well, Coach McBride, perhaps you and I do make a pretty good team," Ginny said.

They turned onto her street. The house was only a block away.

Carter didn't answer, not sure what to make of her calling him *Coach McBride*. He studied her. She challenged him, unlike all those women he tried dating before. They were ingratiating, wanting to fawn over him rather than speak like normal people.

This was better, even if sometimes it was hard.

As they approached her walkway, he paused. Maybe it was time to go for broke.

"So did you get enough stuff done last weekend?" he asked.

Her words stumbled. "Last weekend?"

"Yes. You said it was crazy."

She hesitated again, then slowly said, "I did."

"Are you still interested in a museum?"

She turned her face to him, and his eyes locked on her mouth. He'd thought about kissing it before, of course he had, but now, that moment seemed so *possible*.

He held his breath until she finally answered him.

"Yes. Saturday?"

His chest relaxed. "That sounds great. It generally calms down around five. It takes about forty-five minutes to get there."

"So leave here at four, then?"

Their gazes clashed. He saw more than he'd bargained for in those brown eyes. A vulnerability. Hope. Was all that for him?

"I look forward to it," he said.

Roscoe took that moment to get right between them and sit firmly on the concrete.

"I think Roscoe knows we're planning something without him," Ginny said, cracking one of her beautiful smiles.

He looked down at the dog. "Don't worry, Roscoe. We'll still do plenty of things with you." He glanced back up at her. "Just not this."

Time to exit stage right before he blew it. Carter handed Ginny the tether and took off with a little wave.

Now he had something to look forward to.

CHAPTER 13

Ginny knew she was in for an incredible experience the moment that Carter parked next to the replica of the ship that held the Titanic Museum in Branson.

Their drive up until that moment had been pretty typical for them. They talked about Roscoe and how they might train him next. A little bit about the school. They avoided the topic of his football team, after their discomfort about it on Tuesday.

But as they sat in his truck in front of this amazing building that looked exactly like the historic ship, Ginny leaned forward and pressed her hands on the dashboard. "Is it the same size of the original ship?"

"Oh no. It's about fifty percent. Still pretty impressive."

Ginny couldn't take her eyes off the boat. The

massive chimneys, the portholes, the image that exactly matched her impressions from movies and photographs. If it hadn't been plunked in the middle of the city, surrounded by buildings and trees, she would never have believed it wasn't the actual ship.

She couldn't help but let out a little squeal as they got out of the truck.

Carter laughed. "I'm glad you're so excited. Were you a fan of the movie?" he asked.

"Yes and no," she said. "There were great costumes, and the story was important. But I found some of it a little hard to believe."

"I don't think I've ever stayed awake all the way through it."

"What! They're on a sinking ship! How can you fall asleep?"

"I don't know. I just can."

Ginny shook her head at him, but they smiled at each other as they entered the museum.

As Carter had promised, there was almost no line to purchase tickets. They were each handed a boarding pass that listed the name of an actual Titanic passenger. A woman in a black-and-white servant outfit told them that, at the end of the exhibit, they would find out whether their passenger arrived safely or perished in the waters.

They walked close together as Ginny read about her passenger. She was just a little girl about the age of Ginny's students. She could already feel her eyes welling up with tears. "I hope she makes it," she said. "I don't know if I can take it if she doesn't."

"You have a teacher's heart," Carter said. "It's always nice to see people who were absolutely meant to be in the school system."

No one had ever said that to her. Ginny hadn't intended to be in schools. Most occupational therapists worked in clinics or on a home basis, like she did before. But he might be right. The classroom felt like where she was meant to be.

They walked through the exhibits, touching the frigid iceberg and placing their hands inside water chilled to the temperature that people endured as they abandoned the ship. Carter made it a full thirty seconds before finally pulling his hand out, but Ginny didn't fare nearly as well.

"Good to know what your pain threshold is," Carter teased when she jerked her hand out after only ten seconds.

Ginny shook her freezing hand, and Carter took it, pressing it between his. Her breath caught.

"How is yours already warm?" she asked, trying to keep the tremble out of her voice at his unexpected touch.

"Maybe that's my superpower," he said.

He kept one hand clasped around hers as they walked through other exhibits. A couple employees dressed as crew members described what they were seeing. A room set up as a steerage bunk. Another, larger stateroom. A full model of the entire ship. Despite the grandeur, all Ginny could think about was Carter's hand on hers.

But then they arrived at a wide-open area, and her breath caught.

"This is it," she said.

Carter nodded. "Pretty magnificent, isn't it?"

They stood at the base of the grand staircase from the Titanic. It was a full-sized replica, angel statue, gold plating and all.

Another woman in a crew outfit stood at the bottom. "Go on now, young man," she said. "Go to the top and call to your lady."

"I hope this ends better than their story," Carter said.

Ginny let go of his hand. "It will."

He dashed up the stairs. The woman winked at Ginny and said, "It usually does. Lots of marriage proposals happen here."

"We've just met," Ginny said. "It's our first date."

"You wouldn't know it," she said.

Really?

Before Ginny could ask her why she thought this, the woman said, "Why, I believe there he is." She gestured up the stairs and stepped away.

In that moment, only the two of them stood at the staircase. Carter waited at the top, his brown hair brightened by a light overhead. He grinned down at her, his smile broad and happy. His eyes seemed lit up from within.

Ginny's heart absolutely caught in her throat.

He held out his arms. "What light from yonder window breaks?" he called out. "It is the moon and Ginny is the sun!"

"That's Romeo and Juliet!" she called up. "Wrong storyline!"

"We're not English teachers," he called back.

They laughed their fool heads off like kids making the worst joke ever.

"Come to me, Ginny-et!" He held out his hand.

She ran up the steps, and Carter's arm slid around her waist. This was the closest they'd ever been, his body flush against hers, his hand curved around her hips.

She could barely breathe.

"It's beautiful," she said, gazing down the steps, trying to take it all in.

He turned to look at her. "Yes, you are."

Ginny's throat was so tight, she couldn't say a word. They stared at each other for a long moment, and she marveled at the flecks of green in his brown eyes. Ginny thought he might kiss her, but then a family of tourists arrived, and their children noisily clanked up the steps, breaking the spell.

"Come on," he said. "Let's go find out what happened to your girl."

They headed into the memorial room. Lighted

screens showed the names of all the passengers of the Titanic, their ages, and their fate.

Ginny took Carter's hand and squeezed it.

"Here's mine," Carter said, pointing to a name and short bio. "He was in steerage. Those guys didn't fare too well on this voyage."

"He drowned," she said, reading along, her voice catching. "I wonder what he wanted to be. What he hoped for."

Carter lifted his ticket to the man's name. "Maybe he got a better chance at achieving it on his next go 'round."

"Hopefully so."

The space was dimly lit and hushed. They circled the room, looking for her girl. Ginny wanted to discover her, rather than be led directly to her name. She was eight years old.

Carter leaned close. "I see her," he said.

Ginny followed the direction of his gaze.

And then she saw the name.

She gripped his fingers in a vise as she read, then relaxed. "She survived."

"Look what she became," he said, pointing to the line just past her name.

"A schoolteacher."

Ginny's eyes smarted with tears. The girl had become an orphan, but still gone on to live a happy life. In comparison to that, losing all her family to the unforgiving sea, nothing Ginny had ever been through was difficult at all.

Could Carter see that? Even if some woman had turned him down in front of an audience, he still had a great life to live. She wished she could say this, but he didn't know she was aware of his past. She hadn't watched the YouTube videos, although she'd certainly seen a whole host of links after Googling his name. She'd let him tell his version before she invaded his past.

They examined some of the artifacts that had been rescued from the ship and read about their owners. By the time they stepped outside, their hearts full, twilight had descended.

"You hungry?" Carter asked.

"Definitely," she said.

"Then allow me to buy you dinner."

"I think I will." Their silly grins were back, and neither one of them could stop smiling.

Ginny had to admit that Carly was right. This was definitely a date.

As Carter drove away from the touristy area of Branson to a quieter district, he was glad to be out of Applebottom and prying eyes. He parked, and held Ginny's hand as they walked along the side streets. He led her to a cute little diner with a sign in the window that insisted it was home-style Missouri fare. It was a safe bet, and bore no terrible memories for him.

Branson was his home town, but only good things had happened to him there. Childhood. A stellar high school career. His recruitment to college ball.

The rest was elsewhere.

Ginny paused by the sign. "What would be traditional Missouri food?"

"I'm from here and I don't even know," Carter said. "I grew up on burgers and pizza."

"Your mom not a cook either?" she asked.

"Nope. Although she could order Pizza Hut like nobody's business."

"Mine too."

Carter opened the door, and they inhaled the amazing smell of grilled meat, sauces, and an undertone of sugar. A plump woman in jeans and a flowered shirt gestured them over to an empty table in the front corner by the window. They sat down and looked out on the street. The occasional couple passed by, holding hands and seeming happy.

It was date night, and he was on one himself, finally. He felt hopeful this one would end well, unlike so many before.

The woman dropped off menus and glasses of water. "I'll be right back," she told them.

"You think she's the owner?" Ginny asked.

"I bet so," Carter said. "Little places like this usually have them around on the busy nights."

"Like on Town Square?"

"Exactly. Have you met everyone?" he asked.

"Delilah at the dog bakery, obviously. And two old ladies sat with me at one of the games. They own a pie shop?"

"Gertrude and Maude. They're a pair, that's for sure."

"I was a little intimidated by them."

"They are the unofficial tastemakers of Applebottom. Gertrude's family was part of the original German settlement. Maude's arrived in the eighties. Which makes her an interloper."

"So I'm practically a tourist."

"Me too," he said. "Two years is nothing." He picked up Ginny's hand and circled his thumb inside her palm. He pictured their future walks with Roscoe, able to hold hands now. It was a good step forward.

The woman returned. "What would you two lovebirds like to drink?"

Lovebirds. Interesting. Carter couldn't recall anyone saying something like that on his other dates, not even with Steph, who was beautiful and glittery, but not particularly fond of public displays of affection.

"I'll just keep the water," Carter said.

"You got it," the woman said with a grin. "How about you, honey?"

"Iced tea?"

"Sweet, I assume?" Her tone left no room to argue the point.

"Yes, of course."

She turned away, and they picked up the menus.

"What's most traditional?" Ginny asked. "I haven't been to a restaurant in Missouri since I drove through a McDonald's on the drive down."

"I don't think there's anything quite as iconic as Chicago dogs or Chicago pizza," Carter said. "Missouri's pretty diverse. But looking at what they are offering here, I'd say your best bet for something Missouri-traditional would be the sauced grilled pork."

"That sounds good," she said.

"We'll have to get some gooey butter cake for dessert," he said. "Although I doubt it will be as good as my grandma's."

"So at least you have the cooking gene up there somewhere," she said.

"Oh yeah. Grandma does all the Grandma things. Mom was just focused on her career."

"What did she do?"

"She's a surgeon. Both my parents are."

"How do they feel about you being a coach?"

"Ashamed and embarrassed." He didn't even flinch as he said it.

Ginny's eyes flickered with compassion. "I'm sorry."

"It's okay. I went through an entire period of my life where I apparently disappointed everyone. I'm over it. I like it here. There's no pressure."

The woman taking orders came back over, and they placed theirs. The rest of the conversation was easy and light. Roscoe. Treat bags. Some changes in the discipline code at the high school. Ginny pronounced the pork steak and bacon-fried cornbread absolute perfection.

When the butter cake arrived, Carter lifted it to show Ginny all the gooey layers.

"I think this is going to send me into a food coma," she said.

"I'm glad you liked everything so far. Butter cake, though, is a true test of whether you are meant to live in Missouri." He set the plate between them.

She picked up a fork. They were sharing, after he'd assured her that she might want to try it before committing to an entire piece.

"Well, let's see what my fate is." Ginny carved off a corner of the glaze-laden cake.

Carter watched with bemused interest as she stuck a piece in her mouth. He couldn't wait to see her reaction. Butter cake was the most outrageous sweet thing on any Missouri menu. He rarely let himself indulge in it.

Ginny's eyebrows shot up. Her eyes drifted closed. She made a little *mmmm* sound.

Then she scooted the plate closer to her side. "Forget about sharing," she said. "This is mine."

Carter laughed. He took his fork and pretended to try to stabbing at it while Ginny blocked all his moves. The waitress saw them and hustled over with a grin. "Looks like you might need two of these after all," she said.

"I think so," Carter said.

"I'll fetch it right now."

The meal finished with lots of laughter, and groans, and both of them perhaps regretting they had each eaten an entire piece.

As they walked back to his truck, Carter took Ginny's hand again, this time lifting it to press a kiss against her knuckles. Her eyes caught his, the light dancing in them. This was working. It felt right.

"This has been the most perfect evening," he said.

"Agreed."

He opened her door to his truck, and waited while she slid in the seat. He hesitated for a moment, almost leaning in to kiss her. They'd missed their opportunity on the stairs when a family had taken over the space.

But this wasn't quite it either. Too much noise, people walking around. Not yet.

He pulled back and walked around his side.

On the drive home, they talked of more

Missouri foods as well as ones that Ginny had known from Chicago and Seattle. Every conversation seemed laden with the idea that they had a future, and that one day they would share these other experiences.

Carter felt more and more optimistic that this was working.

But it was just date one. So many of the others had crashed and burned, women acting one way at first, then seeming to want so much so fast. They always had expectations, and he wasn't sure he would ever deliver.

He killed his truck in front of her house. He felt so torn. He wanted to move forward with Ginny. He'd pushed for it even. But even as they sat there, he could picture Steph looking down at him while he got down on one knee. All around him, football players shoved each other and pointed. A cameraman had closed in.

And she'd looked so…disgusted.

He shouldn't have done it. He'd just been so disappointed about not getting drafted. His future had rearranged, the blackness falling in front of his eyes. Steph was there, and she was so perfect and good. He'd wanted to do this part of his plan, even if he had no team to go to and wasn't sure what was next. In his head, some coach would pull him in during the offseason. The draft wasn't necessarily the end.

But Steph didn't believe. She hadn't loved him. She'd loved the idea of marrying a pro player.

And he wasn't one. Not then.

And not now.

They took their time heading up the sidewalk, and Carter forced himself to shake those images away. Why were they coming right now?

Except they always did. Date one, date two, date three. Steph's brutal rejection always inserted itself in the middle. He had to get rid of those pictures in his head.

They made it to her door.

Carter was sure his own mood was spoiled, and he wouldn't be able to focus back on Ginny. Time to punt. Make another run at a romantic moment when he could wrestle his past out of his present.

But then Ginny turned to him, her long hair swinging, her big brown eyes lifting to his.

And everything else fell away. He saw only her and images from the evening. Ginny laughing as she jerked her hand out of the cold water. Tearing up over the little girl on her ticket. Standing at the bottom of the Titanic steps, looking up at him much like she was at this moment.

And this time, it felt right.

He leaned down, his lips brushing against hers.

It was a tentative kiss, almost like a question. His mouth was feather light, the kiss you might expect when you're young and just starting out in love. He was almost surprised by it, its optimism and promise, when he'd felt so jaded just seconds before.

After a moment, Carter pulled back and looked into her eyes. They shone with happiness. "I had a really good time tonight," he said.

"Me too."

"I'll see you on Tuesday? See what we can do with that dog of ours?"

Her eyes glistened a little more with the word *ours*.

And, as if on cue, Roscoe bumped hard against the door.

"He heard us," they both said simultaneously, and burst out laughing.

"I should see to him," Ginny said. "He's bound to be rambunctious."

"All right then. Goodnight."

She paused, looking at him, then stood up on tiptoe to brush another gentle kiss on his lips, this one all her doing.

"Goodnight," she whispered.

She squeezed through the door to prevent Roscoe from escaping.

He whistled lightly as he headed back to his truck, his lips still tingly, his chest puffed out.

This had been perfect.

Life was perfect.

CHAPTER 14

The next few weeks went by in a happy haze. Ginny had more Tuesday-night lessons with Roscoe and Carter where twice her dog succeeded with *stay* when she gave him the command. There were also two more football games, and in one of them, the Eagles actually managed to score a field goal.

She went on a second date with Carter, back to Branson, because there really wasn't much to do in Applebottom. They walked along Table Rock Lake and took in a simple and delicious dinner at a seafood place.

The air grew cold as fall began to give way to the holiday season. Ginny handed out candy to trick-or-treaters, recognizing the children as students from the elementary school, even if they weren't ones who came into her sensory room for occupational therapy. She was becoming one of those citizens of Applebottom who knew everybody.

Ginny even ventured into Gertrude and Maude's pie shop. Maude was there, looking cheerful and sharp in a white apron with their logo stenciled on the front. She served Ginny a slice of their special seasonal pie called Autumn Harmony. It had mixed berries and a strange dark flavor that gave it a savory warmth. Maude told her the secret ingredient was a pinch of curry. Ginny never would have guessed.

She visited Delilah's doggy bakery to pick up more treats for training Roscoe and to thank her for the book. Delilah seemed pleased that they were making progress with Roscoe's manners and had way too many questions about what Carter and Ginny were up to when the dog wasn't around.

Apparently they'd been seen driving together out of Applebottom on two occasions. Plus, they'd taken to holding hands on walks. This town missed nothing.

Homecoming came around. Ginny bought a new bright red Eagles sweatshirt to wear to the game and show support of the home team. By then, she knew quite a few of the faculty members. She sat with Natalie and Carly, and they were joined by some of the teachers from the high school, including the tweedy Andrew McCallister, whom Ginny had run into when she delivered the note to Carter.

She'd heard he was seeing the cake decorator at

one of the shops on the square, and wondered if they had also trouble staying away from the prying eyes of Applebottom. He had asked Carter for advice a week or so ago, a conversation Carter had related to Ginny.

As the game dragged on, the other teachers peppered her with questions about Carter. Everyone seemed to know they were dating—more proof that there were no secrets in Applebottom.

It was clear that the coaches picked the weakest possible opponent for Homecoming in hopes they wouldn't get stomped too hard in front of the alumni who returned to watch the game. Even so, the Eagles were down by nearly thirty points as the game headed into the final quarter.

Carter looked stalwart and strong down on the field. Ginny's heart flipped a little each time she took a moment to really take him in. He wore a ball cap and his red windbreaker over black track pants. He walked up and down the sideline, calling out instructions the crowd couldn't hear. He looked competent and in charge.

Toby, the quarterback, wasn't having a stellar game. Over and over, he struggled to find open receivers.

Ginny had figured out who Toby's parents were. They usually stood next to chain link fence that separated the bleachers from the field.

His mother wore a red jersey with Toby's number

five on it. She layered a turtleneck beneath it so as not to cover it. His father sported an Eagles ball cap and shouted encouragements between plays.

In the last five minutes of the game, a small miracle occurred, and one of the receivers actually managed to catch one of Toby's passes. They were on their own twenty-five-yard line, and the possibility of the first touchdown of the season was high.

The spectators jumped to their feet. Ginny moved out of the bleachers to stand at the chain-link fence, a short distance from the quarterback's parents. She wanted to be near Carter if they did score to see his excitement up close.

They set up the next play, and she really hoped that Toby would be able to pull off a touchdown. As a freshman, he would have a lot of room to grow. He was the sort of player Carter could build around if he wanted.

Not that Ginny talked to him about football. Not after the disaster that one Tuesday night.

The play began, and Toby dropped back, looking for an open receiver. There wasn't one.

His father cupped his hands around his mouth, and yelled, "Just run with it. Toby. You know what to do."

It sounded as though Toby's struggle had been discussed around the dinner table. His father must have told him to defy whatever Carter might have told him to do and make a play on his own.

Now that Ginny was so close to the field, she could see the hesitation in the young player. He had his father instructing him to do one thing, and his coach another.

He threw the ball out of bounds to avoid getting sacked.

His mom looked disgusted. "I can't believe that coach won't allow him to just keep it. They could actually score."

"I know," the father said. "If I could have him on any other team, I would."

The mom gripped the fence. "We'd have to move forty miles away to go somewhere else."

Come on, Carter, Ginny thought. Let the boy have a big moment. Let the team score for Homecoming. She had every confidence he could do it.

They set up for another play. This time Toby handed the ball off and the play ended abruptly when the running back got plowed by the defense. They only had one more shot at moving forward before they would have to attempt a field goal. With the kicker they had, it was unlikely the team would score at this distance.

"Keep the ball!" the dad yelled.

Carter heard him and turned, a flash of anger crossing his face.

Toby missed none of that. Poor kid. He was caught between the two men he admired most.

The teams lined up for third down. Ginny hung

on to the crosshatch of the fence, anxious about how the play would go.

The center snapped the ball to Toby. He dropped back, looking for someone to throw it to. Still nobody.

Keep it and go, Ginny thought. She didn't realize she was yelling it until the quarterback's mom looked over at her in surprise.

Toby tucked the ball under his arm and shot forward. He skirted two defenders and pivoted quickly to avoid another. He made it almost twenty yards before he was brought down on the eight-yard line.

The fans went nuts. The students screamed and jumped in the stands. The band kicked off the fight song. They had four more downs to try and score.

The energy was palpable. Ginny glanced over at Toby's parents, who were whispering to each other. Then she looked out at Carter. He had his hands on his hips. Just as the play clock was about to wind down, he signaled for his players to call a time out.

The boys circled for their instructions. The track put some distance between the stands and the edge of the field, so she couldn't hear what they said.

But she could guess. Toby was looking down at the ground. Carter was gesturing wildly, as if he were angry.

They set up for the next play. With less than ten yards to go, it would make most sense to keep pushing forward with a running play. Trying to pop up a pass with the short distance and their less-than-stellar catching history seemed unwise.

And sure enough, Toby handed the ball off to the running back, who got instantly creamed for negative yards. He was tackled pretty heavily, and the audible *oh* from the stands washed over the field.

The energy would drain quickly this way. But what did Ginny know? She wasn't a coach. And what she did understand about football was heavily tainted by her father's opinions regarding a professional sports team.

She tried to relax, resting her arms on the fence, and waited to see what would happen.

Toby drew back again, almost seeming as though he was going to pass high.

But then Ginny saw his eyes go determined. She knew what he was thinking. She saw the empty space between him and the goal line. Any second, it would fill back in. Any moment, he could be sacked by a defender breaking through.

"Go for it, Toby!" Ginny screamed. Then clapped her hand over her mouth. But his parents heard her, and began the cry.

"Keep it, Toby! Keep it!"

The crowd took up the chant

"Keep it, Toby!"

Carter did not turn to look at the stands. But his hands moved to his hips, and his shoulders tensed.

She could feel the anger wafting off him even from behind.

Toby did what the crowd suggested, shooting forward. He ducked away from the arms of the only defender who had noticed him come through, and crossed the goal line.

The stands erupted into a roar. Ginny glanced behind her, smiling at the students and faculty and parents and fans all hugging each other and shouting. The band struck up with the fight song again, playing with considerably more enthusiasm. The cheer-leaders were only a few feet away, jumping and screaming and crying.

Carter's posture didn't change as the team set up for the extra point kick. No doubt he would hear from a lot of people about the quality of this quarter-back and that he should just let him show off his skill.

Ginny wished she'd kept her mouth shut. She felt torn between her loyalty to Carter and what was obviously good for the team.

But what if Toby could be the catalyst to turn the team around? Hadn't Carter just talked about how a good coach can rally a quality team even as the great players left and new ones came along?

Maybe it was Carter who needed to grow. If she could see it, the principal would be able to see it, and the school board. The other coaches. The people who could hire or fire him. They would all see it.

The kicker, perhaps inspired by the unexpected score, focused in and actually made the extra point. This set off a renewed fervor of cheering and screaming from the stands. There was no chance that they would actually win the game. They were still down by twenty points with only a few minutes left. But numbers on the boards were about as much as they could ask for.

Toby didn't attempt any more quarterback keepers. But the excitement remained high. Toby's parents seemed more or less placated, and they accepted handshakes and well wishes from faculty and students as they filtered past them from the stands.

Natalie came up behind Ginny. "Are you gonna wait for Coach?" she asked.

"I think so."

"See you Monday, then," she said. "Good luck. He should be happy. They scored."

Ginny nodded, her eyes going back to Carter. He followed the team off the field.

She hurried along the chain-link fence to catch up, so that she could see him as he passed by.

What she didn't expect was his dark glare.

Ginny tried to ignore it. "Good game, Coach," she said. "Your first touchdown! It must feel great."

"I heard you," he said. He stopped in his tracks, causing a player who was trailing behind to smash into him in confusion.

The boy walked around him, glancing back and making a grimace at Carter's stony expression.

Other fans and parents crowded up to shake Carter's hand, but he didn't even look at them. His eyes were on Ginny.

"You knew, and you still encouraged him. You encouraged him to defy me. *You.*"

Ginny had to take a step back, the anger coming off of him was so palpable.

"Great game, Coach!" someone shouted. "Keep it up."

"Carter," she said, trying to keep the shake out of her voice. She really didn't want to have this conversation in the midst of all these people. "I'm sorry. I like football. I just shout things. It's part of the game."

"You deliberately got the crowd riled up against me."

Ginny could barely breathe. "I'm sorry," she said again, even though she wasn't totally sure that she was. This whole argument was madness. It was a *football game.*

But not to him.

Ginny took another step back and was swallowed into the crowd, which moved forward to greet the coach.

He plastered on a fake smile and shook their hands and took pictures as requested.

Ginny fell farther back until she couldn't see him anymore.

Her stomach trembled. Carter expected loyalty from her. His job could be difficult. So could Ginny's. Sometimes parents, fellow therapists, colleagues didn't quite understand what you might be doing in a specific case. You counted on those who did understand your methods and the reasoning behind your actions.

Carter had counted on Ginny to be that person. To understand why he instructed his player to do what he did. And she hadn't done that. She had very publicly raised up the cry that Carter was wrong without even asking his reasoning.

Ginny turned and ran to her car. She wanted away from the stadium lights, the people, the happy students excited for how the game had gone. She wanted solitude. Her own four walls. And her dog.

That was all she wanted.

Escape.

Ginny didn't receive a text or a call or any notes in the days after the game. By Tuesday, when she and Carter would normally meet by for the dog lesson, she didn't really expect him to show.

Five o'clock arrived and passed with no knock at her door. Despite the bitter cold, Ginny bundled up and took Roscoe out for the short walk to the park. The dog dragged her up the hill, seeming to know they were supposed to find Carter, and upon not seeing him at the top, let out a desperate howl that struck her to the bone.

Ginny completely understood how Roscoe felt.

They shivered as they hurried back to their house, the heater, and blankets. She didn't even write Carter to ask why he hadn't come.

She knew.

On Friday afternoon, Ginny headed up to the high school as usual. Her feet were heavy. Most of the time, when she arrived, she would stop by Carter's office. He was always there during this timeframe, since the girls had taken over the gym. They would often talk for a moment, or he would help her set up for that day's physical therapy.

She didn't know what to expect from today. Would he make sure he was out of his office completely? Would he stare at her in stony silence? Would there be another confrontation?

Ginny's stomach felt shivery as she crossed the gym and headed into the locker room.

As always, she cracked the door and called out to make sure no students were inside.

She crossed the equipment room and opened the next door to the hallway of offices. The baseball coach was in his, and Ginny gave a little wave. She tried not to be too obvious as she peeked through the windows at Carter's desk. He wasn't there.

She deflated a little. She'd expected this, but it was still hard to see him blatantly avoiding her.

The baseball coach stood up and came to his door. "Looking for Carter? He has a meeting with some of the football parents."

"No, just setting up for my usual occupational therapy."

"Ah, that's right." He disappeared in the other direction.

Ginny opened the closet and pulled out her stability ball and a set of hand weights. She needed to focus back in on her students and what needed to be done to help them.

She sat on the floor, sorting through her notes about Jason, a junior at the high school. He had been diagnosed with a defiance disorder that caused him to explode in anger when even small requests were made of him. They were slowly working on strategies to put some space between the moment when he heard the request and when his body reacted so violently—a bit of time for him to try to engage a coping strategy to prevent his explosion.

Jason wanted to do better. The aftermath of his explosions always brought on fear and self-loathing that they were trying to also address. It wasn't an easy case. He was a big, strong boy, and some of the teachers feared him. Ginny hated that any child had to manage life like this.

As she reviewed her notes, she got Carter so completely out of her head that she didn't even notice someone had walked through until a door clicked down the hall.

She glanced up to see Carter disappearing into his office and closing the door. She had no idea if he had even looked her way. The temptation was strong to go up to his door and force him to talk, but at that moment, the special education teacher for the high school brought Jason in.

Ginny had to begin work. She could only hope that maybe Carter would still be there when she was done.

Ginny worked with Jason, both of them throwing weighted balls at a target to vent their frustration. She got so focused that, at one point, Jason stopped throwing and just watched her.

She turned to him, and they both burst out laughing.

"You seeing a therapist for that anger, Miss Page?" he asked.

"I should!" she said.

They dissolved into laughter again, and she felt that seismic shift that sometimes came when the rapport between her and one of the kids turned into something they could build on. Trust had been established. They were going to make great progress.

The two of them worked on balancing on one foot in increasingly difficult poses, breathing and easing any frustration they felt until the aide arrived with another student and Jason's time was up.

The next two students' work went by quickly. When they were through, the aide talked with her quietly about another potential student who might be added to the roster.

When the aide left, Carter began packing up his things, as if he might escape before Ginny could speak to him.

She left her equipment on the floor and hurried his way.

She wasn't going to give him the opportunity to slink out.

It wasn't that Carter was avoiding Ginny.

Okay, maybe he was.

He just didn't know what to say.

He'd been raised by psychiatrists, who always nitpicked his every move. Dinner conversations often revolved around patients and their mistakes and their resulting loss of potential. Carter didn't miss their thinly veiled attempts to turn those cases into a lesson for him.

This was why football had become his sanctuary. The sides were clear. You had your team, and you opposed the other. Your teammates were everything. They defended you. You blocked for them. And when everyone worked together, plays went exactly right. And you won.

Then football had failed him. And so had love. Or whatever had stood in for love. He wasn't sure what Stephanie had represented. So he'd flailed about.

Until Ginny.

For the first time in years, he'd felt that connection again. Of being on a team. Of knowing somebody always had your back.

Until she didn't.

He was overreacting, and he knew it. But he could no longer relax around her. She'd become another disapproving voice. Like his students' parents. Like his own parents. Like Steph.

And here Ginny was, barreling toward him after working with her students. He had to brace himself. He couldn't avoid her forever, so he might as well face it now.

He stood just inside his office door, his athletic bag over his shoulder.

"Can I help you?" The chill coming off of him could have frozen the ice caps. He knew it, but there was no way to warm up how he felt.

Ginny's eyes were overly bright, as if she was forcing herself to look normal.

She plunged straight in. "I just wanted to say that I was sorry for calling out suggestions to the team that I knew were against what you wanted," she said. "I should've known that your strategy was important to you. Of all people, I should have known."

Well, she understood at least. His jaw clamped down, and his hand tightly gripped the strap of his bag.

She blundered on. "I heard you had a meeting with some of the parents. How did that go?"

"Not so great." He didn't really want to rehash it all. "Excuse me." He tried to brush past her to leave his office.

But Ginny stepped in front of him to block his path. "Now, wait a minute. You can't blame me for parents being upset at you for very clearly preventing a player from using his potential."

"Is that what you think? That I'm preventing his potential?"

"I do," she said. "And now you're acting like I am the devil incarnate. Just because I disagree with how you're coaching your team."

Maybe she *didn't* get it.

"You sound like everyone else, like I'm not worthy." He tried to keep his voice straight, but there was a defeated note in it anyway.

Ginny noticed. "But I don't think that." She hesitated. "And I'm definitely not *her*."

So she knew about Steph. She'd probably watched all the humiliating footage. He'd never, ever escape it. It would live on the Internet forever.

His head felt hollow, and his voice sounded foreign to him. "It feels like history repeating itself. The one good player. The team asking him to carry them. Him failing. Him failing at every single thing."

"Carter, I'm not—" Ginny said, but he interrupted her.

"I study these kids. I know how far they can throw. How fast they can run. I know when they are feeling tired or unsure or just plain defeated. There's more to a team than trying to make one kid a hero."

Ginny's defiant stare faltered. "I get that."

"But you yelled at Toby to do the opposite of what I told him." He tried to move around her again.

But she still stood in his way. "I want to understand. What you're saying is that because I challenged your coaching, that that makes me the sort of woman who will hurt you publicly like your ex-girlfriend did? That's what you think?"

"I don't know," he said. He couldn't keep it all straight in his head. "Maybe."

She let out a long breath. "Then I guess we're done here." She stepped aside to let him pass.

At first, he didn't move. Maybe he was wrong. Maybe he was speaking from some hurt, angry place, and it had nothing to do with Ginny.

But it was done now. Anything else they had to say would just hurt each other more.

So he walked away.

CHAPTER 16

*A*ll afternoon, Ginny couldn't get their argument out of her head. Carter had sounded so disillusioned. He wasn't making sense. He was layering his old trauma on top of his current situation.

She'd seen it plenty. She was a professional who managed traumatized people every day. They relived the bad stuff over and over until it became a part of every moment of their lives. It discolored every experience and tainted every decision.

The town had raised money to bring Ginny to Applebottom. They felt like she had answers that they needed. They hoped that she could help fix balance issues, teach strategies, improve skills, all the way from walking in a straight line to managing a school day without exploding in anger.

But right now, she was failing. Because it seemed to her that the person who needed her most on this campus was the one she cared for above all others—and so far, she hadn't helped him at all.

The football game that night didn't appeal to her whatsoever. It was an away game, and she certainly didn't need to return to the site of the arguments with Carter. It seemed best to just stay away until she figured out what to do.

The next morning dawned cold but clear, so Ginny bundled up and took Roscoe for a brisk walk through the park. Despite the popularity of the playground that morning, with children running in every direction, Roscoe responded to all her commands. He sat. He came when called. He even managed to *stay* when a small child with a peanut butter sandwich got tantalizingly close.

Ginny was so proud of him.

As they walked toward home, she decided to push herself. If she was going to ask Carter to be brave, she would have to be, too.

She was going back to Town Square. Roscoe was having a good day, and it was time to try.

As they turned the corner onto the square, Ginny was amused to see that the battle for the appropriateness of early Christmas decorations was being waged among the shops.

The nail and facial spa was in full Christmas

glory, with windows decked in red and gold and signs for gift cards and holiday pampering.

Next door, Betty at Tea for Two had taped up a hand-lettered sign that said rather strongly that they would *not* be decorating for Christmas until after the Thanksgiving turkey had been carved.

Ginny pictured tiny chic Betty in her pink jogging suit with her matching white poodle sticking her nose in the air when she saw the Christmas decor on the spa.

Delilah's doggy bakery had begun its Christmas transformation, with fluffy snow in the corners of the window, and the outline of *Seasons Greetings* ready to be filled in on the window panes. Thankfully, Nothing but a Pound Dog had its door closed today against the chill. As beautifully as Roscoe was ambling down the street with her direction, she wasn't sure she could trust him inside the bakery again. Not yet.

Better to be cautiously brave than foolhardy.

Next door, the florist was still in full-blown autumn. This made sense, since they would be providing centerpieces for Thanksgiving dinners for another couple of weeks. A gorgeous explosion of brown twigs and red leaves and gold accents filled their window.

Ginny checked out the pie shop, which was firmly in the no-Christmas camp. It did not have a snarky note like Betty's tea shop, but the sign in the window about holiday orders had a big broad stroke underneath the word *Thanksgiving*, suggesting that no one need ask about Christmas yet.

Ginny smiled to herself. It was glorious to live in a town where the biggest argument was about the timing of the Christmas decor.

Other than, maybe, how to handle the football team's quarterback.

She and Roscoe hit their first snag in the slow careful walk around Town Square when a woman left the pie shop holding an amazingly aromatic meat pie. Roscoe came to a halt, nose in the air.

"Steady, boy," Ginny said, firmly grasping his collar.

She reached into the treat bag at her waist to withdraw one of his training snacks. When she placed it under his nose, Roscoe seemed placated and ate the snack willingly.

Ginny sighed in relief as the woman disappeared down the walk, taking her pie with her.

Ginny spotted Gertrude and Maude through the plate-glass window of the shop, looking out at her.

This was her big moment. She fetched another treat from her bag. Ginny reached down to pet Roscoe on the head. "Let's do this, puppy dog." She showed him the new treat. "Roscoe, sit."

Roscoe's oversized haunches landed on the pavement. She stroked his ears.

"Good dog," she said and fed him the treat. "What a good dog."

Maude opened the door and poked her head out. "I can't believe how well he's doing!" she said. "Why don't you tie him to the bike rack there and come inside a minute? I've got a piece of Dutch apple pie with your name on it."

Ginny hesitated. Leaving Roscoe even for a moment seemed like a risk. But then, Maude had accidentally thrown down the gauntlet. If Roscoe couldn't wait a couple minutes like any other dog, maybe she hadn't done as good a job as she was trying to prove.

"Just give me a minute to secure him," she said.

"I'll heat it up for you," Maude said.

Ginny kneeled down in front of Roscoe. "Okay, here's how it is," she whispered. "I've got a blanket and a chew bone. Can you do this for me?"

Roscoe licked her nose. Good enough.

Ginny unrolled the blanket from the tie on her backpack and made a neat little nest on the ground. She tested the bicycle rack and ensured that it was securely bolted to the concrete. It seemed sturdy.

She unhitched the leash from her harness and wrapped it around the rack several times before fastening it down. She withdrew a thick rawhide bone for Roscoe and set it on the blanket.

Roscoe immediately plopped down and began gnawing on the bone. He seemed all right.

Ginny stood up. "Good dog, Roscoe."

She would eat the pie, chat up the ladies, and get out as quickly as she could. And then she would have proven her point.

The shop was warm and full of amazing smells. Ginny caught a whiff of apple, spice, berries, pumpkin, and mincemeat. She realized how much she had run around and walked with Roscoe all morning without eating. This would be amazing.

Maude placed a warm slice of pie on the counter in front of a stool. It looked like a magazine worthy slice, from the expertly crimped crust edge to the perfectly placed mound of ice cream.

Ginny sat down rather deliriously. Maude leaned against the counter across from her, brushing aside a nonexistent crumb.

Her dark eyes twinkled as she watched Ginny devour the first few bites of pie. "I like a girl who can eat," she said.

Gertrude loaded a chocolate pie inside the glass case and slid the door closed. "I expect that's because you want everyone to pack on the same extra pounds you have," Gertrude said.

Ginny's fork froze in mid-air. Was Gertrude always this nasty?

But Maude just laughed. "Gertie, if you had any more padding you wouldn't be able to fit behind the counter."

So this was just how they communicated. Ginny

took another bite and observed both of them. Neither of them were large women by any stretch. Gertrude was somewhere in her late sixties or early seventies. Her hair was white and puffy around her perpetually frowning face. Her apron was streaked with pie filling and caked with flour.

Maude, on the other hand, looked crisp in her perfect white apron that set off the golden tones of her dark skin. She had a kindly look of a favorite grandmother, but Ginny guessed she was probably about ten years younger than Gertrude.

Gertrude picked up a pie with a fluffy white meringue and lifted it by the palm as if considering whether or not to aim it at Maude's face.

"You wouldn't dare," Maude said.

"And why not?"

"Because that's the lemon meringue you make every morning in case Alfred Felmont comes by for a slice."

Gertrude sniffed and lowered the pie. "So what if it is."

"He's not interested in your ugly mug."

Gertrude lifted it again. "Might be worth it today."

Never a dull moment around here.

They remained poised in their standoff another few seconds, then Maude shook her head and picked up a rag. She wiped at the counter as if it wasn't already cleaner than a tea kettle.

Gertrude set the pie on the counter. "Maude, you

know you dragged that poor girl in here to ask her twenty questions about whatever the hell happened at the football game last week. So just get to it."

Maude sighed. "Nobody ever accused Gertie of being subtle."

"It's Gertrude. You'd think after thirty years you'd get it right."

"You'd think after thirty years, you'd realize I'm never gonna call you Gertrude."

The argument rolled off their tongues like a well-polished stone, repeated over the years until all the rough edges were gone. Funny how some people spoke to each other like this all the time. From what Ginny understood, these two were the grand dames of Applebottom.

And they wanted to know about her situation with Carter. As if she could explain it.

Gertrude popped the first hard question. "So what in the world caused Carter to go off on you in front of everybody? Has he lost his mind?"

Ginny slid her fork across the empty plate, trying to scrounge up any last crumbs. "Maybe I just know a little too much about football."

Even with her eyes down, she didn't miss the glance that passed between Gertrude and Maude.

Now they both leaned against the counter.

"Let me get this straight," Gertrude said. "Carter went ballistic on you in front of everybody over *football*?"

"Right," Ginny said.

"Got to be more to it than that," Maude said.

Ginny stared at her plate. "I wasn't loyal."

Maude stood up abruptly. "Loyalty! That boy doesn't have enough years on his bones to know anything about loyalty. You two have had what? Two dates? I'm calling his mother."

"Can it, Maude," Gertrude said. "His mama ain't from Applebottom."

"She's from Branson, and that's close enough. It's Missouri. I want to give her a call."

"Please don't," Ginny said, feeling all of fourteen years old. "He's an adult man."

"Then he needs to behave like one," Maude said. "You don't go talking down to a lady who's taken an interest in your occupation. It's not seemly. And if you do find yourself crossways with her over an issue, you certainly don't hoot and holler in public during the Homecoming game. That's when all of Applebottom, past and present, are supposed to come together."

Gertrude turned the pie around and around on the counter, as if examining the meringue for flaws. "Just listen to yourself, Maude. You're going off like a preacher during Lent. Ginny here has him figured out. He expected more from her. I'm telling you, he's still got a hold on him from that city girl."

"I'm a city girl," Ginny said. "Seattle born and raised. Then Chicago. This is my first small town."

Maude tapped the counter in front of Ginny. "And you've fit in just fine. We haven't heard a negative word about you since you arrived. Well, other than that dog. You got all the mamas in town praising your name. Why Jason's mama was in here just yesterday, and said that he was behaving like a normal kid for the first time in his sixteen years. Did you know that woman hasn't had a moment's peace in her life since that boy was two years old?"

Tears sprang to Ginny's eyes. "That's good to know," she said. "He's been doing really great."

Maude squeezed Ginny's wrist. "Two months," she said. "Two months you've been here, and you got Jason to think about things before he explodes. You got Delilah's grandson running on the playground again. He wouldn't do that for years, afraid of falling down. And we ourselves saw little Amy Eaton at Annabelle's Cafe, using a spoon rather than her fingers."

Gertrude nodded. "Seems to me that if anybody's going to help Carter, it's going to be you. Don't you let a little bit of anger set you off the path."

Maude picked up the plate and fork and turned to set it in a dish basin behind the counter. "We won't call his mama. We expect you to get in there and help him out."

"He helped you with that brute dog," Gertrude said. "It's time for you to use that big city expertise, and help him right back."

Ginny wasn't sure she could do that. But looking out the window and seeing Roscoe still lying in his blanket nest chewing on a bone, she realized that they were right.

She owed it to him to try.

Ginny spent the rest of the weekend going through everything she knew about self-esteem in both adolescents and adults. It wasn't her area of expertise. She had always focused on occupational therapy in kids. But so much of what they practiced in children could easily be scaled up for adults.

The trouble was, did she know Carter well enough to do anything to help? And how would her efforts be received? He might be insulted by them. Or he could just simply blow them off.

She wound up making two separate trips to Branson. No doubt half the town was watching her every move. She couldn't count on Applebottom's attention span being short enough to forget about the fight between the new therapist and the football coach, even if it had been a week ago. Although looking at the rather simple items she had bought, probably no one would be able to put together the ideas that Ginny had for Carter.

She needed an ally over at the high school to help her pull all this off. Preferably someone with keys to every room.

The trouble was, each school had its own set. There weren't many people who could get into any location in the high school, who also came over to the elementary where she could forge an alliance.

When Ginny got to work Monday morning, she stopped by the front desk to talk to Mrs. Humphries. If anyone would know who could get into Carter's office, it would be her.

She would have to handle the conversation carefully, though. If Mrs. Humphries got even a whiff of what Ginny was up to, the whole town would be all over the situation and her strategy might not work at all.

Mrs. Humphries reminded Ginny of the principal from the movie version of *Grease* with her big pearl earrings, broad-shouldered suits, and the perpetually pinched expression that suggested she disapproved of everything.

She had been the elementary school secretary before Ginny was born. The only person who might rival the information in her head would be the high school secretary, Sadie.

"How can I help you, Ginny dear?" Mrs.

Humphries asked, patting the hairpiece that quite clearly filled out the thinness of her steely gray updo.

"Do any of the custodians work at the high school as well as here?" she asked.

Mrs. Humphries eyes shined as if Ginny had just offered up a glamorous new piece of gossip.

"Whatever would you need a custodian at the high school for?" she asked.

"Well, I do have some duties over there as well as here," Ginny said smoothly. "And there's a closet there that holds many of my things. I'd like to start locking it, but I don't have a key."

Mrs. Humphries cast her eyes down in disappointment. "Well, Mr. Farley specializes in the heating units at all three schools," she said. "He can get into pretty much any room or closet on any campus."

"Thank you so much," she said.

Her eyes sparked again. "Did you have a way into the closet before? Perhaps a person who is no longer so willing to...assist?"

"Oh no. I'm just moving some things after hours, and Sadie isn't there to call someone for me."

Mrs. Humphries's expression collapsed again. Poor thing, just looking for a little tidbit to send on down the gossip line.

Ginny turned and headed out. She knew Mr. Farley. He was the perfect ally. Quiet, discreet, and—unlike Mrs. Humphries—not the least bit nosy.

It was a whole week before Ginny got any indication that the things she'd left for Carter might have had any sort of impact. She had just left the building to check on Roscoe, when someone called out, "Miss Page!"

Ginny stopped. A high school boy in a football jersey ran up. She didn't recognize him, but then she didn't know the team super well—just Toby, the quarterback, and a few of the receivers. They were mostly a blur of indistinct faces, hidden by helmets.

"Hello," she said. "Can I help you?"

"I need to ask you something."

"You're on the football team?"

"Yes. And coach assigned us something, and I thought maybe you would know what I should do."

Ginny's heart sped up a little. What had Carter done?

"What is it?"

The boy slid his backpack off his shoulder and unzipped the front compartment. "I think you see my little brother Tommy," he said. "In your special room with all the balls."

Ginny spotted the resemblance. Both boys had a smattering of freckles across their cheeks, and coarse reddish-brown hair.

"I do. Are you Frank? Tommy talks about you all the time. He really looks up to you."

"That's cool," he said sheepishly.

"Why are you over here at the elementary?"

"I'm in that program where we read to the kindergarteners."

"Oh! How nice. What did you need help with?"

When he whipped out a section of fabric cut into the shape of a superhero cape, Ginny had to hide her smile.

"When Tommy saw this, he said that you had done something like it with him."

Frank was right. The superhero cape was a strategy she had not used often, but it was perfect for what she was trying to do with Carter and his team.

"I think I have done that once or twice," Ginny said carefully. "So what are you doing with one?"

"Coach said that we should write our super-powers on this cape. I have no idea what to put on mine and the team meeting is right after school."

He held out the cape. "I don't know what to say on mine."

"Well, what are some things you do well?"

"I don't know. I just sit on the bench. I don't tackle very well. I'm not that great of the catcher. Not fast."

"That's okay. Try not to think in terms of what you can't do. What made you start playing football to begin with?"

"Because my dad made me?"

Ginny bit back a smile. She was used to these

sorts of answers. Small town, big city. Parenting was often the same.

"Go beyond athletic skills," she said. "There's a lot more to football than that. There's planning. Team building. Supporting and encouraging your teammates."

Frank stared up into the sky. "Well, whenever the water boys don't show up to practice, I always make sure the igloos are filled up, and we have enough cups."

"There you go, perfect. You would write *I pitch in wherever needed.*"

"Okay. And hey. When James was all busted up about not being able to play on his hurt ankle, I sat with him on the sideline."

"Excellent. So you're supportive when other people are feeling down, and you encourage injured teammates."

"All right! That's three things. I only needed three things."

"I bet on the way back to school you'll think of some more," Ginny said. "Sitting alone in a car will really open up your head and let you think."

"Okay. All right. Thanks." He shoved the cape into his backpack and turned back toward the lot.

"You're welcome!" Ginny wanted to ask him about the assignment, and what Carter might've said to them about it. But he'd already jumped into his car and fired up the engine.

As she walked home for a briefer than usual visit with Roscoe, Ginny had to smile to herself. Carter might not have done the assignment she had given him himself, but he saw something in it that was useful for his team. Maybe that was a good second choice.

To get direct to Carter, she would have to up her game.

She already had lots of ideas.

CHAPTER 18

Carter sat in his office after school, looking at the newest thing Ginny had sent over to him. He assumed it was her. Nobody else would have done it.

Clearly, she had someone at the school helping her get things in his office.

It didn't matter. The team building stuff she'd sent had been very helpful. The guys had totally dug the superhero capes exercise, even though they were skeptical at first. And the work they had done on setting goals and focusing their efforts on their strengths had been a good way to organize his somewhat rambling talks, as well as their practices. It particularly helped the captain of the team. He was headed off to college next year, and he was learning skills that would definitely be useful for the long-term.

Ginny was definitely an asset on all that.

But this new stuff was a lot more personal. He hadn't given it to his team.

He fingered the poster board titled *Happiness List*.

What made him happy?

This team, for sure. He really believed what he said about it not being about winning or losing. It was teamwork. Loyalty. And one of the things that he knew he'd done well with his boys was to keep them loyal. They would support each other. And if they had criticism, they kept it inside the team. And constructive. Nobody tore anybody else down inside his organization.

What else made him happy?

He remembered those walks with Roscoe, particularly the calm he and Ginny had felt after helping her dog in the storm, looking out over the park in the rain.

He'd loved the sense of absolute accomplishment when Roscoe finally started to click to the commands. Then there was the laughter and sheer relief that they were actually doing something right.

But none of those things were really about Ginny. They were situations. Those situations could have occurred with anyone.

The meetings he'd had with parents since Ginny had roused them all at Homecoming were unlike anything he'd ever experienced. It made him question everything, and even wonder if he should move on to some other school.

He rested his head on his hands. What a mess.

He kept staring at the happiness list.

What made him happy?

Maybe he wasn't looking deeply enough. Maybe he ought to be looking for more.

Dodge, his assistant coach, poked his head in. "You up for Old Man Football? They're assembling outside."

He'd forgotten. "Give me a sec to change."

"See you out there."

Carter shoved the happiness list partway under his desk calendar and grabbed his duffle bag. The Old Man Football league was one of the responsibilities he'd inherited when he came to Applebottom to coach.

Mostly the league existed to extend the real or imagined glory days of some of the old players. Archie, the game announcer, always suited up, even though he was all of eighty years old. And Fred, the chief of the volunteer fire department, always showed and often dragged a few of the others from the fire crew out.

T-bone sometimes played too, and it was pretty comical to see the mayor out of his leather vest and motorcycle boots, wearing sneakers and a jersey.

Once Carter was in his own shoulder pads and practice jersey, he tossed his bag back in his office and paused. He remembered those jerseys he and Ginny had found. He dug around in her closet and found the box, leaving the banners behind. When he carried it out onto the field, Dodge was already out there, directing the others in a warm up.

He set the box on the bench. Nearby, Micah was warming up with kicks in the sideline net. He had a leg on him at least. He was the town lawyer now, and played in high school a decade or so ago. He was at the younger end of the group.

The old timers didn't always bother with pads. They were content to stand out there and catch the odd pass, maybe run a few yards. The only people who got tackled with any force were Dodge and Carter.

Carter ran out on the field to toss passes to a line of receivers, a favorite part of the warm up, which often lasted longer than the scrimmage. When it seemed that everyone who was going to come had showed up, he grabbed a handful of jerseys from the box. "Got something fun," he called out. He passed them out, red shirts for one side and blue for the other.

"Hey, this was my number," Archie said, holding up the number five.

"You were a quarterback?" Carter asked.

"I was. Class of 1958." Archie tugged the shirt over his head. Without shoulder pads, it fit fine.

"You should keep it," Carter said. "Bring it next time."

Archie didn't take his eyes off the jersey, stroking the number on his chest.

"Where'd you find these, Coach?" asked Micah as he pulled on a blue jersey.

"In a closet. Some had gone to rot."

Micah straightened the top over his pads. He intended to actually play.

"You sure your tender lawyer bones can handle a tackle?" Carter teased.

"You bet they can."

Micah jogged out onto the field. He was about Carter's age, but he'd grown up here. He might be someone to ask about Ginny and what the hell to do.

Carter lined up the teams, serving as quarterback since someone needed to call the plays. Dodge led the other side.

The afternoon cooled as they ran down the field, passing and grunting and laughing at their own incompetence. Micah kicked a field goal, and Archie carried the ball for a touchdown.

Carter watched the men, faces alight with exertion and shared memories. They seemed to revel in the feeling that nothing great was ever truly lost.

As the game wound down, Micah stood next to Carter. "This sure makes these old men happy," Micah said.

"It does."

"Thanks for continuing the tradition."

"How long has this been around?" Carter asked.

"My dad did it," Micah said. "And I've been out of school twelve years."

"You should get more of the young people out," Carter said.

"They're busy," Micah said. "Marriage and kids and all that."

"Not you, though."

Micah shrugged. "My girl didn't want to live in Applebottom. My parents needed me here. So we parted ways."

That was remarkably close to Carter's story, other than the public humiliation part. "Nobody around here's caught your eye?"

"I'm up to my neck in my dad's mess," Micah said. "I heard you snagged that new girl, though. The OT."

Carter looked out over the field. The old men were still talking about their glory days. "We dated a while. We didn't see eye-to-eye on my job."

Micah turned to him. "She doesn't like that you're a coach? You're like the king of the town, other than maybe T-bone over there."

"No, the job is fine. Just not how I'm doing it."

Micah pulled off his helmet. "Well, doing a public thing like coaching football has its critics, that's for sure." He laughed. "Was she right or was she wrong?"

Carter kicked at a tuft of grass that had been

displaced. "She was probably right. But I blew up about it."

"Is she worth trying to fix it?"

"Probably."

"Then fix it."

"No clue how to do that."

A ball sailed near them, and Carter reached up to snatch it from the air. He tossed it back to Fred, who gave him a shout of thanks.

"Nice catch," Micah said. "I'm sure you'll figure it out."

"That makes one of us."

"Just go big. Sounds like you need a Hail Mary. I bet you're good at those." Micah gave him a little salute and took off for the locker room.

With his departure, the bulk of the players started heading inside as well.

Carter collected jerseys to be washed. A couple more of the regulars held on to theirs and he let it go. They'd earned them.

He looked out over the empty field. In football, a Hail Mary was a long throw, one you could only pray would land in the right player's hands to save the game. It was a long shot, the play you made when you really had nothing left to lose.

As he picked up the box to follow the men inside, he wondered what his Hail Mary play with Ginny could actually be.

And even if he figured it out, whether or not he'd have the guts to try it.

On Friday, Ginny's heart almost leaped out of her chest to see a note from Carter in her box. She snatched it up greedily.

She knew he must have gotten all the assignments she'd sent him. Some were very personal, asking about the things that made him happy and creating a calendar of favorite moments, both past events and future hopes.

As disappointed as she was about his reaction to her opinions about football, she hoped some of them included her. This was fixable. Would he want to fix it? *Could* he?

Ginny couldn't wait to go to her room to read it. She had to do it now. Would he apologize? Say he'd be there Tuesday for the dog lesson? Maybe ask her to the Harvest Dance?

But it was none of that. As Ginny scanned the words, she slowly realized it was just a thank you note for all of the team building exercises she had sent.

Her stomach fell to her shoes. He thought she was doing it out of professional courtesy. Even the personal stuff. He didn't get it. Not at all.

Or didn't want to.

Ginny arrived at the high school that afternoon with a heavy heart. She assumed she wouldn't see Carter. The note had made it clear that they had a different sort of relationship now.

When she stepped into the equipment room, an easel in the corner held a board covered with sticky notes. At the top was the title *Short-term goals*.

Ginny walked up to it.

Some of the goals were obviously geared toward the game.

- Complete five passes.
- Learn a new fake handoff play.
- Perfect the onside kick.

But a few others were more about the team.

- Fire up Simon before each punt.
- Find a better position for Devin.
- Get Marcus more playing action.
- Talk to each other on the field.

Ginny plucked an extra sticky off the pad in the corner and wrote *take more risks*. She stuck it near the top.

She moved on to the offices. Carter's was empty, but they all were. No one was in the locker room at all.

She peeked in his window. Sitting on his desk,

right in front of his chair, was a small poster board she'd had Mr. Farley leave there. At the top were the words *Happiness List.*

And Carter had put quite a few things on it.

Ginny pressed against the glass, trying to read it upside down in the half-dark.

1. My team. They have heart.

2. The school. It fosters camaraderie.

3. The community. They support and finance us.

There was a fourth, but it was partially obscured by a play binder.

What did it say?

Ginny thought she saw an R and an O. Roscoe? Or was it a P and A? Page? Her? Ginny Page?

Her face was so close to the window, she fogged the glass.

A door in the equipment room opened. *Oh*! She smeared the steamy spot off the glass and dashed past the offices to the dressing room.

She dropped her bag on a bench and hustled to the closet door.

Locked. That was strange. Normally it was just open.

She glanced over just in time to see Mr. Farley coming her way.

"You asked for a key," he said.

Ginny forced her breath to slow down. At least it wasn't Carter catching her spying on his list. "Thank you," she said.

Mr. Farley bent his tall, wiry frame to peer at the lock on the closet door. He seemed lost in the over-sized navy jumpsuit with the Applebottom logo over the pocket.

When he had opened the door, he turned to hand her a key. "Just making sure it worked. Can't get you one for the locker room without the principal's say so, but if the building's open, you can get in your closet."

"Thank you." She stuck the key in her pocket. "That's very helpful."

"And on that other matter," he said with a wink, "he got all the supplies you sent over."

"Thank you extra for that."

"He's been working on that last one for days," he said. "Burning the midnight oil."

"Which one is that?"

"The happiness one."

"Oh. Good."

"Not a happy man right now, I 'spect." Mr. Farley said, straightening to full height. He twitched his mustache. "Hopefully you can set him straight. I hear you're good at that."

"Well, I'm not sure about that, at least not with Coach," she said.

Mr. Farley took a few steps away, then turned back. "I probably shouldn't say nothing, as it isn't my business."

He hesitated, and Ginny wrapped her fingers

around the key, breath held.

"He made that calendar you sent."

"Did he?" Her heart was about to pound out of her chest.

"Your name was on it. I wouldn't say nothing about it, 'cept I figure somebody ought to know if somebody's writing their name on a calendar."

"Was it a…past date?" she asked. "Or future?"

"Didn't look that hard to know," he said. "Just saw your name, that's all."

Ginny's student came in just then, and Mr. Farley hurried out.

As Jason started in on his first routine, a set of balance moves to help him manage frustration and set his focus, Ginny's thoughts turned back to Carter.

He might have put her (or Roscoe) on his happiness list. And he definitely put something about her on his *Favorites* calendar. He had taken all her suggestions for activities for team building, expression, and self-esteem.

Even though he hadn't mended their rift in any way, they were still connected.

It would have to be enough.

CHAPTER 19

Speaking at the Last Ditch was a tradition for the head football coach of Applebottom, but Carter wasn't sure his heart was in it.

Last year, he'd been fortunate enough to catch the flu, and Dodge had done it. After a year of dating random women in the district, the last thing he'd needed was to spot their hopeful faces in the stands for the biggest surprise-date event of the year.

The Last Ditch was not his favorite Applebottom tradition. It was connected to the Harvest Dance. No one knew exactly how it started. The land around Table Rock Lake was forested and rocky, not conducive to crops whatsoever.

But still, there was a Harvest Dance and to top it off, both students and the community at large were encouraged to create the most outlandish proposals imaginable to convince the object of their affection to be their date.

It no longer mattered which gender asked whom. But as the dance neared, the town became littered with signs and temporary monuments chronicling attempts of the citizens, young and old, to secure a dance partner.

One week prior to the dance was the final pep rally, which included the Last Ditch. Anyone who had not yet succeeded in finding a date for the dance could walk to the microphone and ask someone in front of the whole school as a grand gesture of courage.

The cheerleaders ran out to the center of the gym floor in a blur of cartwheels, and the band cranked up. Carter glanced down the line of football players to be sure everyone seemed all right. Probably more than one of them would attempt a last-ditch proposal.

The team filed onto the bleachers. The pep rally portion would happen first, and then at some point the Student Council president would arrive to start the Last Ditch. The event was capped at half an hour, so that an endless stream of students couldn't to keep it going just to get out of class.

The band played the school song and the fight song, and the cheerleaders danced. George, the captain of the football team, strode out to give a rousing speech about victory, not that it had ever happened in his years.

Carter willed himself not to look out into the stands to spot Ginny, even though he knew she'd be there with the elementary school kids. All the schools sent their students over for the pep rallies to foster Applebottom spirit.

He found her anyway, sitting along a row of kids who looked pretty uncomfortable to be there. More than one wore brightly colored headphones to muffle the noise.

A little guy, probably not even seven years old, stood up and tried to bolt. Ginny neatly caught him and pulled him next to her, reaching into a bag at her feet to give him a squishy pink pig to squeeze. He settled down with it, and she looked up.

And their gazes connected.

He gave her a curt nod. He'd appreciated all the things he'd sent for the team to do. The superhero capes had gone over well. The priority lists. It gave them something to focus on as they closed out a losing season.

The happiness list and favorites calendar had given him some pause. He'd done a little work on them and set them aside. Thinking too much about the past or future made him uncomfortable. He was good right here, thinking only about what was right in front of him.

All the seniors were called down to the floor to be

honored. More than one teacher could be seen sniffing as they listed the kids who were in their final year.

Carter would be losing six players. He switched his attention to them, giving them an encouraging nod.

Finally, a lanky boy in jeans, suspenders, and a bow tie approached the mic stand.

"I'm Bernie Owens," the boy said into the mic. "And I'm here to get us started with the Last Ditch."

A roar rose from the crowd.

Bernie glanced at his watch. "We have a limited amount of time. So if you're thinking of inviting that special person to the Harvest Dance, you better get on down here and be ready for your public humiliation."

One of the percussionists began a drumroll.

Everyone swiveled their heads to see who would be the first to brave the potential social embarrassment of the Last Ditch. But no one came forward.

"Anyone? Nobody this year?" Bernie called out.

Carter had watched one of his players sweating it out, and knew he was thinking about doing a Last Ditch. Carter shifted behind his chair and pushed him on the back.

It worked. Barry stood up and started out to the center of the gym. A great cheer rose up.

Behind him, one of the players said, "I think he's going to ask Amelia."

Despite his initial reluctance, Barry seemed fine when he got up to Bernie. He took the mic off the stand and swung the wire around like he was an experienced showman.

"Good afternoon, Applebottom High!" he called. "I'm Barry, and today I'm here at the Last Ditch to ask a very special girl to attend the Harvest Dance with me."

Another cheer erupted from the crowd. When it died down, he went on. "I was supposed to plan this whole big thing, but some coach over there"—he aimed a finger at Carter and waited out the laughter —"had us in practice too much this week. So here goes."

Carter shook his head, arms crossed. He'd probably be called out more than once today. That was one of the things that came with teaching high school kids.

"Hannah Malvern," the boy called out, dramatically holding out one of his arms, "will you do me the honor of attending the Harvest Dance?"

In the stands, a few people let out a gasp. Everyone looked around for this mysterious Hannah. At first no one stood up. Carter spotted a bit of a commotion farther up the stands. A blond girl was being nudged in every direction, her face as pale as milkweed.

"Go, Hannah, go!" several people said. One tried to grab her hand and drag her to standing.

The poor girl was mortified.

But Carter could have told her that Barry wouldn't give up. He'd seen the boy play.

"I know you don't like standing up in front of everyone," Barry said. "But we've been studying together for three weeks, and you saved my grades, and this team that was about to have to do without me." More laughter. "I want everyone to know how amazing you are."

The girl looked like she might be getting braver. Finally, she stood up.

The entire gym erupted in cheers.

Down on the gym floor, Bernie took over the mic. "Come on down, Hannah," he said.

Hannah made her way down to the gym floor. Barry took her hand. "So is it a yes?" he asked.

Hannah nodded.

Another great cheer went up.

Bernie lifted the mic. "Success! Who's next?"

This time two more guys and a girl came forward. They lined up beside Bernie.

"Ladies first," Bernie said, handing the mic to an athletic girl with her hair twisted up in a messy bun.

"All right, everybody," she said. "You guys all know that I've been after one guy since sophomore year, and I've never done anything about it. That ends today."

A chorus of whispers broke the quiet. From one far corner, a chant began. "David, David, David."

The girl pointed at him with a smile. "You got it. David Warner, get on up here. Because I'm asking you to the Harvest Dance."

A tall awkward boy with a massive curly head of hair stood up. He pointed at himself in the chest as if to say *Who, me?*

Bernie took the mic. "Come on down here, David. Don't make us come get you."

David jumped down from the side of the bleachers and headed to the center of the gym. Bernie held the mic to his face. "So what you say?"

David leaned in. "But I don't dance."

The girl grabbed the mic. "I can teach you."

David nodded to that, and another cheer rose up.

The next two boys came, both with success. That was typical. A school-wide audience was the ultimate peer pressure.

Another member of the football team lumbered up to Bernie. Dudley hadn't played more than a few minutes that season, although Carter had tried to encourage him to go in a time or two. He was timid. Several of the players had been more or less pushed onto the team by their parents. Applebottom wasn't big enough to have tryouts, so everyone made the team.

"Another mighty Eagle about to spread his wings!" Bernie said. "It's Dudley McPherson!"

Dudley didn't take the microphone from Bernie, but simply leaned in. His faced turned bright red as he said his words as fast as possible. "Jennifer Lightsey, will you go to the Harvest Dance with me?"

A gasp came from the cheerleaders. A tall brunette with a giant red bow in her ponytail opened her mouth in shock. The other cheerleaders stood near her, hands clasped to their cheeks.

Clearly this was unexpected.

Jennifer backed away from the group until she bumped into the wall. Then she took off for the door and slipped out.

The gym sat quiet for a long moment. Dudley hung his head.

"Sorry, Dudley," Bernie said. "It was worth a shot." He turned back to the stands. "Anyone else?"

Carter glanced back over at Ginny. She leaned in close with another teacher, both seeming concerned about Dudley's rejection. The gym murmured.

Dudley still stood there, looking forlorn and lost. He cut his eyes toward the team, and his expression sent Carter straight back to the day of his failed draft and even bigger failed proposal. His throat closed up.

No one had stood with him that day. He'd had to wind his way through cameramen and announcers and players and coaches and team reps. Alone.

That was not happening to Dudley. Not on his watch.

He would not stand alone with his rejection.

Ginny's heart leapt when Carter headed toward the center of the gym. He was still looking at her.

Why was he going to the mic while looking at her?

Carly leaned in. "What's he doing?" she asked.

"How am I supposed to know?"

Her heart thudded even harder. Carly squeezed her hand. Something was definitely up. People were looking from the coach to her, and murmuring.

Was Carter going to do a Last Ditch himself? Was he going to ask her?

Maybe that was why he had sent Ginny the note. To break the ice. To let her know he wasn't upset anymore.

Ginny knew exactly what the students were going through. She felt hot and cold at the same time. The possibility that she would throw up was real. She clasped her hands tightly together, trying to keep herself under control.

"Hey, Applebottom!" Carter called out.

"Hey, Coach!" the crowd shouted back.

"I'm up here to stand with Dudley," Carter said, gesturing toward his team. "It's not easy to come up here and get turned down." He glanced at the cheerleaders, still missing one of their members. "Or to do the turning down. It takes a lot of courage."

Applause broke out across the gym.

Ginny felt her stomach start to drop. Carter wasn't doing a Last Ditch. He was just supporting his student. She tried to rein in her disappointment.

Carter waved at his team. "Come on over here. We'll stand together with Dudley."

The players ambled over from their chairs. Carter waited for them to settle around him, then went on. "We've been working on becoming a stronger team. Along the way we learned a lot more about each other and what our strengths are. We all even made capes."

At that moment every member of the football team unfurled their superhero capes and fastened them around their necks.

Ginny sucked in a breath. Her capes!

"I wanted to talk about somebody who's made a real difference to our team in the last week or so." His eyes searched the crowd, but didn't land anywhere in particular.

Was he going to actually talk to her in front of everyone? At the Last Ditch?

Bernie must've had the same question, because he leaned over and said, "You do know this is the Last-Ditch portion of the pep rally, right, Coach?"

"I do," Carter said. His voice reverberated through around the gym, and straight into Ginny's chest. "One of the things that we learned this week was to recognize when we had made mistakes, and to try to fix them."

Carly reached over and squeezed her hand. Ginny's stomach started flipping again. This was worse than any roller coaster she'd ever ridden.

"I wanted to have a very special Last Ditch today. I know that the Harvest Dance is traditionally a couples dance where people pair off and attend together. But this year I wanted to welcome everybody to the dance. Whether or not you worked up the courage in the last few weeks to ask someone. Whether or not you feel like you fit in or don't. I want to see you there next weekend. And if you don't have anybody to dance with, come to me and we will all dance together."

A great cheer went up and Carter gave the room a strong nod.

And then he walked away from the mic.

Ginny's heart fell. She'd done exactly what she set out to do. She'd helped them forge a stronger team. She'd made Carter see beyond the rejection he got a long time ago. It had led him to try to help others, like Dudley. He'd changed the Harvest Dance for the better, right there in front of everyone.

But it hadn't helped her at all. Nothing had changed between her and Carter.

It really was over.

CHAPTER 20

Ginny sincerely regretted signing up to chaperone the dance. Even though she had not endured humiliation anything like poor Dudley at the Last Ditch, she still had this negative feeling come over her every time she thought about the pep rally.

Carly offered to come over and get ready together. Ginny took her up on it, because she really needed to be with a friend, no different than if she were going into the dance as a high school student without a date, despite what Carter said.

Ginny surveyed her flat, dull hair and wondered why in the world she thought Carter would ever have been interested in her at all.

They only had two dates. She laughed at herself in the mirror. "You didn't even get a third and out."

But she *had* gotten the kiss. That made her at least a little bit different.

Carly came over around six. The chaperones were due at the dance at seven. Ginny felt she was mostly ready. She'd pinned part of her hair back and stuck a couple rhinestone clips in it. And she actually had makeup on.

But the moment Carly popped in and saw her, she said, "Oh no. That will never do."

She immediately started pulling the combs out of Ginny's hair, and looked around the bathroom until she found a curling wand to plug in.

"It's not like it's my dance," Ginny argued. "Let the girls outshine me."

"This is not a high school dance," Carly said. "This is a *community* dance. I want that jerk football coach to see how beautiful you look and feel regret all the way to the tips of his crummy little shoes."

This made Ginny laugh.

Of course Carly would look stunning with her long blond hair in loose curls and a shimmery dark gold dress that perfectly conjured the idea of autumn and the harvest.

Ginny's navy-blue bridesmaid dress still hung on the hook by the door.

Carly examined it. "This is pretty. I don't think I ever had a dress from a wedding that I wore again."

"It was a really posh affair."

"You must have some fancy friends back in Chicago."

"Not really. One of them just came from a rich family. She was super sweet herself."

"Curling iron is fired up and ready." Carly walked across the bathroom and instructed Ginny to sit on the stool.

For the next twenty minutes, she worked magic on Ginny's shoulder-length hair, curling it in spirals that Ginny never could have managed on her own.

When she finished, Ginny looked like a dark-haired Goldilocks.

"So is this some new look I don't know about?" she asked.

"We're not done, dummy," she said. "Now we need the epic brush out."

Carly ran through the curls for what felt like an hour, using her hands to control the hair as it slid through the bristles. Ginny tried not to think of Carter, whether he would dance, or how she would feel to see him there. She had a job to do. Chaperone the kids and go home.

As Carly sprayed something fruity on her hair, Roscoe trotted up and sniffed the air.

"What you think, Roscoe?" Ginny asked.

His nose continued to move from side to side, then he left the room.

"Quite the critic," Carly said with a laugh. She

whirled Ginny around on the stool to face the mirror.

Ginny had to look twice. Her hair was glorious, straight out of a magazine. She thought it would most certainly be stiff and difficult to manage, but every curl was bouncy and soft.

"What voodoo is this?" she asked.

Carly smiled at her in the mirror. "Like it? You look amazing."

"I look like a movie star."

And she did. It was actually a great feeling. As Ginny slid on her dress and a pair of pretty shoes, she knew Carly was right. Let Carter see her like this and wonder if he had made a mistake.

They loaded up in Carly's car to drive over to the high school. The dance would be set up in the cafeteria, one of the few spaces in Applebottom big enough to hold a dance.

When they stepped inside, streamers crisscrossed the ceiling from wall to wall, and a big archway of balloons led up to the stage at the end.

But the curtains were still pulled, hiding the actual platform. A long banner was strung across the curtains, reading, *Surprise Decoration to be Revealed.*

"That's interesting," Ginny said to Carly. "Is it always a secret?"

"Not usually," she said. "But you never know. Each year is different."

They walked along the perimeter of the cafeteria,

looking over the refreshment table. Half of it was taken up with lines of small water bottles.

"No more punch bowls to spike," Ginny said.

Carly laughed. "Did that ever actually happen? I think that's something that only comes up in movies."

"An urban legend," Ginny agreed. "Do we have to make them all dance at arm's length?"

Carly spun one of her long blond curls around a finger. "The kids will be fine. It's the adults we'll have to watch."

Carly and Ginny sat on chairs along one wall as the students started filtering in. Soon, adult members of the community also began to arrive. While the teens were shy and stuck to the edges of the room, the older citizens sauntered out to the center, dancing up a storm.

Within an hour, the event was in full swing.

A teen girl jumped up on stage and dragged a microphone to the middle. She flipped it on, and a roar of feedback made her step aside for a moment, but then it receded.

"Hello everybody!" she called out, then waited for the general rumble to quiet. The music wound down and finally stopped completely.

"I'm Sabrina Mavis, and I'm the head of the Harvest Dance Committee at Applebottom High." She paused to wait out the smattering of applause.

"We use the Harvest Dance to celebrate a successful school year as well as a thanks to the community and staff at the high school." She paused again for more clapping.

"Now, it's our big moment. Tonight, we will reveal a special set constructed by our football team as part of their team-building exercises. To talk about that, we have our own Coach McBride."

The girl backed away from the mic, and Ginny's breath caught as Carter hurried up the few steps to the stage.

She wondered if she would always feel this way about him, and if seeing him would always make her heart give a little flip.

This was why people didn't date people they worked with. She and Carter had barely done anything, just a couple dates and some dog lessons, and here she was mooning over him like a teenage girl.

His eyes took in the room, and Ginny thought he paused on her for just a moment before moving on.

Carly leaned in. "He *definitely* just looked at you."

Carter cleared his throat.

"Welcome everybody. The gym looks great, doesn't it?" The room broke out in applause again, and this time, a few cheers. Several of his football players whistled loudly.

"Before we show you the hard work of our team, I

wanted to thank all of you guys for supporting us this year. We had some real talent on the field."

More applause.

"I bet you want to see the decor! Last weekend, since we had a bye week, the players got together to create something special for tonight. It was the perfect creation to work with Sabrina's Ocean of Stars theme."

He paused for a moment, his mind momentarily blank.

Could he do this? What had he planned to say to them?

To her?

A few people cleared their throats. He could feel his heart pounding.

He forced himself to go on. "One of the most important things we learned during this period is that if you make a mistake, you fix it. Tonight, I'm hoping to make a little progress on that."

He found Ginny, and their gazes caught. She was watching.

She looked so different, her dark hair down and curled. And in a dress, long and blue. She looked elegant. And perfect.

They stared at each other so long, with him still not speaking, that several members of the crowd followed his gaze to look at Ginny. He could see their nods and their understanding from the edges of his vision.

One of his team members—Joey, he'd bet—shouted, "Just show us the stage!" Several people tittered.

"Will do," Carter said, breaking free of Ginny's gaze and letting his eyes glance through the crowd. Nobody was talking or looking anywhere but at him.

"Recently, I had an amazing night with an amazing person. And I wanted to re-create that moment tonight." He picked up the mic stand and moved it to the side of the stage. He nodded at the girl waiting, her hands on the ropes to the curtains, and she tugged until they opened.

Carter couldn't see Ginny right then, as he was turned to the stage, but an audible sigh fell across the audience.

They had done well. His senior boys stood in suits on a replica of the steps of the Titanic.

As everyone clapped for the beautiful set, Carter turned to find Ginny again.

He could see her eyes glistening even from this distance, and her hands were clasped together in front of her nose.

"Miss Ginny Page, would you do me the honor of being the first to walk up the steps?"

Now the whole town turned to look. Her friend Carly gave her a little push to move out of her chair.

She stood. The crowd began to part to let her through.

As instructed, the football players walked off the

stage, two of them heading toward her to escort her to the steps. She seemed a little unsteady and smiled at them as they each took one of her arms.

They led her up to Carter, and he took both of her hands in his.

"Third date," he said quietly. "I had to make it a doozy."

She swallowed before she could respond. "You did."

The music started up again as Carter led her to the base of the staircase. It wasn't a million-dollar construction like the one at the museum. But the wood was stained, and the sides painted gold. Anyone who knew anything about the movie or the ship would recognize it.

They took the steps one by one up to the top. Then they turned and looked out upon everyone in Applebottom. A great cheer rose up. A photographer moved into place, his assistant setting up lights on either side.

"I wanted to ask for your forgiveness," he said. "And to thank you."

"You didn't have to—"

"No, I did. I was stuck in my past. Only when you forced me to consider my life now and what made me happy did I figure it out."

"I'm glad you did."

They grinned at each other like foolish teens. Carter felt his stomach begin to settle. She wasn't mad. This was going to be okay. He hadn't blown it completely.

Carter leaned in close. "I guess it would be totally inappropriate for me to kiss you in front of all these impressionable young people," he said.

Ginny nodded. "Probably so."

But then someone from the crowd shouted, "Stop your yacking and kiss her!"

Carter spotted a man in a long beard, sleeveless shirt, and a leather vest. His arms were outstretched. Of course.

As people recognized who had called out, they took up the cry. "Kiss her! Kiss her!"

"Who is that?" Ginny asked Carter. "Does he even live here?"

Carter chuckled. "That's T-bone. He's the mayor. And I believe he has just issued an official city proclamation."

He turned Ginny to face him. The whoops and the cheers drowned out the music as she looked into his eyes.

He leaned in, and the kiss he dropped on her mouth was the gentlest, and quite possibly the most chaste, of their relationship.

It was also the sweetest. As the approval of the crowd washed over them, Carter realized that those people had made this happen.

Maude and Gertrude and Delilah and the school

secretaries and Mr. Farley. Even the mayor. The whole dang town.

They were his team. They had led him to Ginny and Roscoe. Kept them together. And then when he'd messed it up, they'd helped her help him.

Applebottom itself had brought them together.

CHAPTER 21

The winter afternoon proved bright and clear as Ginny and Carter walked Roscoe from her house to the park. A few squirrels ventured out, digging at the base of trees for their buried nuts, and Roscoe lunged forward.

"Roscoe, heel," Carter commanded.

Ginny stifled a giggle as Roscoe snorted out his nose, his one protest to being told what to do, but he obeyed, walking alongside Carter, the leash slack between his collar and Carter's hand.

Ginny felt so free. Gone was the harness around her waist. They'd given that up between Thanksgiving and Christmas.

And with a new book from Delilah's store, they'd taken a fresh approach with Roscoe at the New Year, and this one had worked much better.

They crested their favorite hill and paused. Down

below, parents were taking advantage of the good weather. A dozen of them ringed the playground, their children shrieking and running amok.

Two women in scarves and long coats approached, their heads down in deep conversation. Only when Maude looked up, her friendly face breaking into a smile, did Ginny also recognize Gertrude.

"Who's watching the pie shop?" Ginny asked when they got close enough to hear her.

Gertrude rolled her eyes. "This crazy partner of mine convinced me to hire some help for a few hours so we could take a walk around the park in daylight."

"It's beautiful out today," Carter said. He tightened his hold on Roscoe's leash to make sure he didn't act up in front of the old guard of Applebottom.

"If you like turning into a freezer pop," Gertrude grumbled. "Have I had enough fresh air yet?"

"Not even close," Maude said. "You need your weekly constitutional."

"I'd rather be at the shop."

"Alfred Felmont is in Branson today," Maude said, tucking a loose bit of her red scarf into place. "So you're not missing him."

"I'll have you know that I didn't even make a lemon meringue pie today," Gertrude said. "And stop meddling with that scarf. You're as fidgety as a mouse."

Carter and Ginny glanced at each other and hid

their smiles. Those two never would stop sniping. Carter had suggested Ginny send them some therapy assignments, but she wasn't crazy. The pair most certainly knew they were perfect exactly as they were.

"Good to see the two of you looking so happy," Maude said. She let go of Gertrude to pet Roscoe's head. "What a good, handsome doggy."

Roscoe lurched forward as if he would put his paws on her shoulders, his favorite greeting, but Carter kept him down. "Stay, Roscoe," he said.

The Great Dane snorted in disgust, and Maude burst out laughing. "He sounds just like Gertie when somebody doesn't finish their slice of pie!"

"Oh, hush," Gertrude said. "Come along. Let's not rain on their love parade."

The two women moved past them to head down the hill.

"To the lake?" Carter asked.

"Sounds lovely."

They circled the playground, the happy shouts of the children already making Roscoe jumpy and itching to run loose. As they reached the opposite side of the mass of parents and children, they spotted Delilah underneath a small portable tent shade.

"What's she doing?" Ginny asked.

A couple with their German Shepherd moved aside, and they spotted a sign hanging on a white table.

Dog treats! Support the middle school soccer team!

"Oh boy," Ginny said.

"Roscoe can handle it," Carter said.

"Are you sure?"

The other couple bent down and fed their dog something from the table.

Roscoe stopped dead, watching the exchange. He looked up at Ginny as if to say, *Where's mine?*

"Might want to feed him something," Carter said.

Ginny fumbled in her backpack for a treat. She had quit strapping the special bag to her waist when they'd given up the harness.

The couple with the German Shepherd walked closer. The woman still held half of one of Delilah's signature dog cookies.

"You want to say hi?" the woman asked her dog.

Roscoe lunged again.

"No!" Carter and Ginny both called out at the same time.

The woman looked startled, but she steered her dog a different direction.

"Please say they're not locals," Ginny said to Carter.

"Definitely not," he said.

Delilah noticed them. "Hello, Carter! Hello, Ginny!" she called. "How's that big doggy?"

Roscoe strained against the leash. Carter doubled it up in his fist.

Delilah held up one of the dog cookies. "Come get a treat for that big handsome boy."

"That's okay!" Ginny called. She could see the Carter's hand turning red from the cinch of Roscoe's leash. They had to get him out of here.

But Roscoe had seen the cookie. He lunged to the right, knocking Carter off balance.

Ginny squealed as Carter stumbled, the leash unwinding from his fist.

"Don't let go!" she called, leaping for Roscoe's back.

But they were way too late.

Roscoe took off. The leash jerked from Carter's hand. Before they could even call his name, he had torn down the path toward Delilah.

Her eyes got big as he approached.

Ginny sprinted like she had never done before, reaching, trying to grasp the end of the leash, which bounced over the dead grass like a hyperactive snake.

Delilah backed away as Roscoe reached the table, leaping right up on top.

By the time Ginny arrived, he'd knocked over three jars of treats and vacuumed up all the samples. He jumped down and began eating the spilled cookies as fast as he could. Plastic baggies filled with dog bones slid in a cascade onto the ground.

"No, Roscoe!" Ginny shouted, grasping his collar and pulling him back.

Carter arrived, and between the two of them, they

managed to separate Roscoe from the disaster he'd caused.

Delilah's hands pressed against the sides of her beehive, the dog-bone shaped bow on one side completely askew.

"Oh no! The fundraiser!" Her face puckered. "We're trying to raise money for a trip to St. Louis!"

They wrestled Roscoe back onto the path, and Ginny straddled him, her arms around his neck. "Oh, Roscoe," she said. "How could you?"

Carter pulled out his wallet. "Here," he said to Delilah. "Hopefully this will cover it." He handed her a sheaf of cash.

"I can't take your money." She started picking up the packaged cookies. "It's not as bad as it looks. Maybe twenty dollars' worth."

"Then here," he said. "Let me cover it. For the trip."

She accepted a few bills. "Poor dog. And he was doing so well."

Roscoe let out an enormous burp and lay down in the grass.

"Need a nap now?" Ginny asked him angrily. She looked over at Carter in despair.

"I think your doggy treats are Roscoe's kryptonite," Carter said. "Maybe that can be your slogan. 'Makes even the best-behaved dog go bonkers.'"

She laughed. "Thank you. There's always a bright side, isn't there?"

"If he hadn't ransacked your store last year, you wouldn't have made me come help Ginny."

"The best bright side," she said, her face beaming. She righted her treat jars. They were still half full. "It's worth a few lost cookies."

Carter strode back over to them. Roscoe's eyes were drooping.

"I bet you're tired." He took the leash from Ginny and looped it back around his hands. "Come on, you big lug. Let's walk it off."

After a short resistance, Roscoe lumbered to his feet. He looked longingly back at Delilah's table, but when Carter told him to heel, he did.

"You okay?" he asked Ginny.

Now that the moment was over, she had to laugh. "I am. Thanks for covering the damages."

"I guess there are some things even a well-trained dog can't resist," he said.

Ginny threaded her arm through Carter's. "I think there are things nobody can resist."

His face turned to her. "I know exactly what you mean."

The team surrounded Carter on the field. Fourth quarter. The team was down by three points. Three lousy points.

"We can do this," he said. "Applebottom High hasn't won a game in five years. But this is it."

Eleven faces looked at him, mud-streaked, tired, but determined.

Toby leaned in. "We going to do the special play?"

Carter nodded. "Let's surprise them."

Everyone stretched an arm toward the center, hands piled together.

Carter put his on top. He pushed down, and Toby said, "Ready, BREAK."

They flew apart and the team ran back on the field.

The Eagles had just used their last time out.

Carter glanced back at the stands.

Ginny stood at the fence with Toby's parents and her friend Carly. Carly's distended belly glowed like a moon in a white shirt. Her baby was due before the Harvest Dance. He had noticed how often Ginny looked longingly at her friend.

Win or lose, he would do it tonight.

Carter turned back to the field.

A roar rose from the stands. He tuned it out and focused on the players. Robbie bent over the ball, ready to snap. They were running down the play clock a bit. The ball was on the seventeen. At worst, if this play didn't work, they could kick and end the game in a tie.

But if Toby could punch it through, the Eagles could actually win this thing.

Carter gripped his clipboard. The evening was warm for autumn and a trickle of sweat ran down his back. It was just the third game of the season and things were looking awfully good. Even if they didn't win this one, there would be more chances. The team had never worked together better.

Robbie snapped, and Toby took control of the ball. He handed off to Jason, a new addition to the team, who had signed up based on Ginny's suggestion after his improvements last year. He was a solid running back, sometimes bludgeoning his way down the field out of pure will. He circled past a loose defender and crossed back to Toby, invisibly returning the ball to the quarterback.

Nobody would see that.

Jason had brought down enough linemen during the game that they raced for him, anxious to tackle him in negative yard territory.

Toby slipped right through the hole in the line.

A safety noticed—too late—that the quarterback was headed toward the end zone. The race went on, and right at the one yard line, a fast player managed to catch up and leap through the air to bring Toby down.

But it wasn't enough. Toby's shoulders—and, more importantly, the ball—crossed the goal line.

The refs signaled the touchdown.

The noise was tremendous. A funny feeling washed over Carter. It wasn't pride. Or even the thrill of the score.

It was connectedness.

He felt like a part of those boys, an instrument within the team, not in charge of it.

The players converged on Toby, slapping him on the back and lifting him in the air. This was their moment.

Carter glanced back at Ginny. She was crying, the backs of her hands swiping at her eyes.

The cheerleaders were going wild, and the band scrambled to pull themselves together enough to play the fight song.

"Okay, boys!" he called out. "We still have an extra point to kick."

Some of them laughed, as if just realizing they were still in the game.

They set up for the play. Josh had gotten a lot better since last season. Carter still couldn't expect him to do much past the thirty-yard line, but he could handle an extra point.

They lined up, made a clean snap, and Josh sliced it through the uprights.

Another cheer rose up, and the band began the fight song a second time. Carter didn't think he'd ever heard it twice in a row.

He glanced back over at Ginny. She and Carly were both crying now. A lot of the football parents were.

He glanced at the clock. One minute and five seconds.

The offense ran off the field, and the defense went out. There was enough time for the other team to score again, although Carter doubted they had a hurry-up offense good enough to pull it off.

Still, he shouted instructions, gave hand signals, and reminded the team to hang on to their lead.

The defensive line held them through all four downs and into the punt. With only ten seconds left on the clock, Carter instructed Toby to just hang onto the ball and let the clock run out.

Ten seconds until his big moment. And not just the win.

He glanced up at the press box. His friend Archie

was up there. He'd been calling the plays as the announcer since 1990. He'd just missed the heyday of the Applebottom Eagles golden football years. He had repeatedly told Carter at Old Man Football that he thought they were about to get there again.

Maybe he was right. Regardless, Carter had ten seconds until Archie would help him out.

The ball snapped, and Toby hung on to it. The entire stadium on the home side counted down the clock seconds. When the buzzer sounded, Toby dropped the ball, and the team all jumped on each other again.

Carter ran out to be with them. A forty-five-game losing streak had come to an end. The teams lined up to shake hands, and Carter went out to greet the coach for the other team.

Harold congratulated him, seeming pleased even though his team had lost.

As the opponents filtered off the field and into their dressing room, the Eagle team turned around for the school song.

No one had left the stands. The bleachers were filled to the brim with students, faculty, and the townspeople of Applebottom.

Carter took it all in. Everyone was right here. This was it.

As the song wound down, Carter walked up to one of the refs. "I need to borrow your microphone," he said.

Jonathan, the ref, had been working Applebottom's games all four years since Carter had been coach.

"Is this for what I think it's for?" he asked.

"Probably so."

He unclipped the radio pack and handed it over. "Good luck."

The announcer stopped everyone from leaving the stands. "Hold on, folks. We have a special presentation on the field. Everybody look toward the fifty-yard line."

Toby ran up. "You doing it, Coach?" he asked.

Carter nodded and flipped on the mic. "This thing on?" he asked. His voice reverberated from the speakers.

Toby motioned a bunch of his teammates over to the fence where Ginny stood. It was a long way down and around to get onto the football field, so a bunch of them quickly climbed the side and jumped over. The fence was only chest high.

Carter took a deep breath and spoke into the mic. "Boys, could you help my lady onto the field?"

Ginny let out a little squeal as four of the boys lifted her up and passed her over to the other side, where the rest of the team brought her back down.

They escorted her to the fifty-yard line, where Carter stood, not sure his voice was going to work.

He took another steadying breath.

"Come on over here," he said, holding out his hand.

Ginny broke away from the boys, her head tilted as if to ask, *What are you up to?*

Soon they stood next to each other, square in the center of the field.

She leaned in. "Are you about to credit me for this win? Because it was all you."

Carter hesitated for a moment, trying to get past the lump in his throat. She looked so happy, loose bits of hair blowing out of her ponytail, bright and supportive in her red Eagle sweatshirt. He shook his head and cleared his throat.

"Ginny, win or lose, tonight was the night I was determined to do this."

She looked at him with a puzzled expression.

He pulled a ring box from his jacket pocket.

When he got down on one knee, the entire stadium jumped to their feet.

"Carter?" she whispered.

The crowd all started shushing each other so they could hear. Carter waited for the silence.

"Ginny, you're one of the best things that has happened to Applebottom, and definitely the best thing that has ever happened to me. I know I'm just a lowly football coach, but I'm the football coach of the greatest team in the United States of America."

The crowd roared at that, and it took another minute of shushing before they quieted down again.

Ginny laughed and nodded in agreement, although he could see tears in her eyes.

"Ginny Page, would you do me the honor of being my wife?"

For a moment, she just looked at him, and he thought the moment would stretch out forever. Had he been wrong? Was she not ready yet?

But then she held out her hand. "Yes," she said, her voice quivery. The mic couldn't quite pick her up, so the only one who heard it was Carter.

He slid the ring on her finger, and that was when everyone knew her answer.

The crowd went nuts again, and Carter stood up to pull her into his arms.

Flashes went off, and he knew a thousand cell phones were trained on the two of them. But he lifted her chin so that he could look her straight into her eyes.

"We are going to be so happy," he said.

"We already are."

And despite the fact that they were probably going to go viral on social media tomorrow, he kissed her. And not a chaste little kiss as he had done on the steps of the Titanic at last year's Harvest Dance. But a real kiss. The kiss of a husband, sealing a decision to make a woman his wife. A kiss that says forever, for better or for worse, for wins or for losses, as long as they both would live.

Carter did it!

I hope that no matter how big a mistake or over-reaction you might make in life, you're ready to find the Hail Mary play that makes things right again, even if it's a long shot.

Don't miss the wedding of Carter and Ginny, as witnessed by hard-talking, curmudgeonly Gertrude! Fans who receive text or email messages from Abby receive an exclusive bonus epilogue of the wedding for every book!

Sign up to get it!

If you loved the advice the handsome young town lawyer Micah gave Carter at Old Man Football, read all about the romance between Micah (hint: he's a volunteer fire fighter!) and Lorelei in *The Irresistible Spark*.

GERTRUDE AND MAUDE'S RED SLICE PIE

(Perfect for a Harvest Dance.)

CRUST

• **Your best top and bottom pie crust, unbaked**
(Gertrude, aren't you going to give them your secret pie crust recipe?)
(*No.*)
(But, Gertrude, what will they do?)
(*That's why God made the Internet.*)
(But Gertie, it won't be YOUR pie crust.)
(*Exactly, Maude. My recipe is mine. Why don't you give them YOUR secret pie crust recipe?*)
(Ladies and Gentlemen, I suggest you Google a flour-based two-crust pie.)
(*Ha, I thought so.*)

FILLING

• **1 1/3 cup brown sugar**

• **3 tablespoons flour**
(But Gertie, last time you made this pie, it was a little runny. Shouldn't we suggest a bit more flour?)
(*Only if it's raining out.*)
(Oh, right. It was rather humid that day.)
(*Carry on.*)

• **1 tsp cinnamon**
(*I actually just shake it over the fruit until it feels right. You can't go wrong with cinnamon so have at it.*)

• **7 normal-sized plums**
(Gertrude, what is normal sized?)
(*I don't know. Not stingy tiny ones, and not great giant ones. It doesn't matter. Cut them until it looks like it will fill your pie plate.*)
(Oh, that's a good idea. You can always add more.)

• **10 ounces cranberries**
(But Gertrude, a normal bag is 12 ounces. Shouldn't they just dump them all in?)
(*Maude, you're making me as bitter as cranberries with your questions. Sure, they can dump extras in if they want. They can leave them out if they want. It's their pie!*)

• 1 tsp orange zest (I just zest straight into the bowl, three one-inch sections.)

(Finally, a sensible instruction from Gertrude.)

(*Run for the hills, everyone. Maude just paid me a compliment and the sky is coming DOWN.*)

• 1/2 tsp lemon juice

INSTRUCTIONS

1. Preheat the oven to 375°F.
2. For the crust: Lay the bottom crust into the pie pan. Place a half-dozen small cuts in the bottom so it will cook evenly.
3. For the filling: Remove the pits from the plums and slice them. (*I leave the skins on*

but this is a great debate. You bet it is.) Place the sliced plums in a bowl.

4. Add in the cranberries. (*10 oz or the whole bag, whatever suits you.*)
5. Mix the fruit with the brown sugar, flour, cinnamon, lemon juice, and orange zest.
6. Spread the filling onto the crust in the pie plate.

1. Layer the top crust over the pie, cutting slits for ventilation. For our pie, we cut hearts out and place the removed heart pieces on the edges at Valentine's Day. We change the design to stars for Fourth of July or Christmas trees for December. It's a terrific pie for any holiday that needs something red. We brush the top of the pie with egg whites before baking.
2. Bake the pie at 375 degrees for 20 minutes, then cover the edges of the pie to avoid

burning. Bake an additional 20 minutes. Depending on how you decorated your crust, you may need to bake it slightly longer or shorter to avoid over browning.

Enjoy your pie and don't miss more of Gertrude and Maude in the next Applebottom book: *The Irresistible Spark* !

- *The Sweetest Match*
- *The Perfect Disaster*
- *The Irresistible Spark*

with many more planned!

www.ingramcontent.com/pod-product-compliance
Lightning Source LLC
Chambersburg PA
CBHW050847190726
48286CB00007B/2263